The City In FreeFall:

The Wingman

The City In FreeFall:

The Wingman

By Jay. P. Hartman

Published by IngramSpark, La Vergne, Tennessee

2021

Cover by Emily Hartman

One Ingram Blvd., La Vergne, TN 37086.

ShadowQuillsInk is an official imprint of IngramSpark. IngramSpark is unaffiliated with ShadowQuillsInk.com in any capacity and this work does **not** constitute cooperation between the two companies.

Edited using ShadowQuillsInk.com. ShadowQuillsInk is an affordable editing service geared to provide quality service to writers with the aim of providing the resources necessary for fledgling writers to achieve publication. Find out more by going to ShadowQuillsInk.com on any social media platform or by going to www.ShadowQuillsInk.com

This book is a work of fiction. Any references to any persons both real or imagined should be considered coincidental unless specified by the author.

This one is for:
Eric Garner, George Perry Floyd, Breonna Taylor,
Patrick Lynn Warren Sr., Vincent "Vinny" M. Belmonte, Angelo Quinto, Andre Maurice Hill, Casey Christopher Goodson Jr., Angelo "AJ" Crooms, Sincere Pierce, Marcellis Stinnette, Jonathan Dwayne Price, Dijon Durand Kizzee, Rayshard Brooks, Carlos Carson, David McAtee, Tony "Tony the Tiger" McDade, Dreasjon "Sean" Reed, Michael Brent Charles Ramos, Daniel T. Prude, Manuel "Mannie" Elijah Ellis, William Howard Green, John Elliot Neville, Atatiana Koquice Jefferson, Elijah McClain, Ronald Greene, Javier Ambler, Sterling Lapree Higgins, Gregory Lloyd Edwards, Emantic "EJ" Fitzgerald Bradford Jr., Charles "Chop" Roundtree Jr., Chinedu Okobi, Anton Milbert LaRue Black, Botham Shem Jean, Antwon Rose Jr., Saheed Vassell, Stephon Alonzo Clark, Dennis Plowden Jr., Bijan Ghaisar, Aaron Bailey, Charleena Chavon Lyles & her Unborn, Unnamed Fetus, Jordan Edwards, Chad Robertson, Deborah Danner, Alfred Olango, Terence Crutcher, Terrence LeDell Sterling, Korryn Gaines, Joseph Curtis Mann, Philando Castile, Alton Sterling, Bettie "Betty Boo" Jones, Quintonio LeGrier, Corey Lamar Jones, Jamar O'Neal Clark, Jeremy "Bam Bam" McDole, India Kager, Samuel Vincent DuBose, Sandra Bland, Brendon K. Glenn, Freddie Carlos Gray Jr., Walter Lamar Scott, Eric Courtney Harris, Phillip Gregory White, Mya Shawatza Hall, Meagan Hockaday, Tony Terrell Robinson, Jr., Janisha Fonville, Natasha McKenna, Jerame C. Reid, Rumain Brisbon, Tamir Rice, Akai Kareem Gurley, Tanisha N. Anderson, Dante Parker, Ezell Ford, Michael Brown Jr., John Crawford III, Tyree Woodson, Dontre Hamilton, Victor White III, Gabriella Monique Nevarez, Yvette Smith, McKenzie J. Cochran, Jordan Baker, Andy Lopez, Miriam Iris Carey, Barrington "BJ" Williams, Jonathan Ferrell, Carlos Alcis, Larry Eugene Jackson Jr., Kyam Livingston, Clinton R. Allen, Kimani "KiKi" Gray, Kayla Moore, Jamaal Moore Sr., Johnnie Kamahi Warren, Shelly Marie Frey, Darnisha Diana Harris, Timothy Russell, Malissa Williams, Noel Palanco, Reynaldo Cuevas, Chavis Carter, Alesia Thomas, Shantel Davis, Sharmel T. Edwards, Tamon Robinson, Ervin Lee Jefferson, Kendrec McDade, Rekia Boyd, Shereese Francis, Jersey K. Green, Wendell James Allen, Nehemiah Lazar Dillard, Dante' Lamar Price, Raymond Luther Allen Jr., Manual Levi Loggins Jr., Ramarley Graham, Kenneth Chamberlain Sr., Alonzo Ashley, Derek Williams, Raheim Brown, Jr., Reginald Doucet, Derrick Jones, Danroy "DJ" Henry Jr., Aiyana Mo'Nay Stanley-Jones, Steven Eugene Washington, Aaron Campbell, Kiwane Carrington, Victor Steen, Shem Walker, Oscar Grant III, Tarika Wilson, DeAunta Terrel Farrow, Sean Bell, Kathryn Johnston, Ronald Curtis Madison, James B. Brissette Jr., Henry "Ace" Glover, Timothy Stansbury, Ousmane Zongo, Alberta Spruill, Kendra Sarie James, Orlando Barlow, Nelson Martinez Mendez, Timothy DeWayne Thomas Jr., Ronald Beasley, Earl Murray, Patrick Moses Dorismond, Prince Carmen Jones Jr., Malcolm Ferguson, LaTanya Haggerty, Margaret LaVerne Mitchell, Amadou Diallo, Tyisha Shenee Miller, Dannette "Strawberry" Daniels, Frankie Ann Perkins, Nicholas Heyward Jr., Mary Mitchell, Yvonne Smallwood, Eleanor Bumpers, Michael Jerome Stewart, Eula Mae Love, Arthur Miller Jr., Randolph Evans, Barry Gene Evans, Rita Lloyd, Henry Dumas,

and everyone else in the Black Lives Matter movement killed by police brutality.

For six months in 2020, I watched helplessly as the world I created here came off the page. This story is a prayer that we will never again see these tragedies come to pass; that we will never make these mistakes again.

And that you will find your Wingman to guide us all to a better tomorrow.
-Jay. P. Bloodworth (04-07-2021)

The Wingman

There's an instant, right before you fall, where the whole world is moving around you. Your brain doesn't know what's happened yet, and at that moment, you're not falling. But then… *you realize.* Your brain just knows in this instant, *something happened*, you tripped… or something gave way… then comes the panic, the terror. In one instant, you feel nothing. And in the next, you're falling.

I'm falling too… It just took me a little longer than most to figure it out.

My name is Sam Farsight. And for the last twenty-three years, I have been living as the vigilante superhero known as the Wingman. You've probably heard of *him*. As a black vigilante, I have a… *reputation* in these parts. The day I found out I had wings was the happiest day of my life… and the worst. Most kids dream of flying. They imagine feeling the wind blowing across their bodies, they long to reach up and touch the soft, fluffy clouds. And beyond that, to the stars. But I never did… No, I've always been afraid of heights.

You can't believe everything the papers have said about me! I've done a lot of things—some of them I'm more proud of than others. But I've always tried to *save* lives. Not all of it was my fault. I didn't mean for those people to die—and I certainly wasn't involved with the Nuclear Swap! No sir! I stayed the hell away from that fiasco.

I've always tried to be better than the villains I put away… It's just… sometimes things don't always work out. I've made terrible mistakes. But. What I have to tell you today should make up for all of them!

I need your help. Normally, if I need something done I'd just do it myself. That's the kind of man I am. It burns my gut to ask anyone for *anything,* but… well, I've got other things burning me at the moment—bigger things. You see, today is the day I'm going to die. Strangely enough, this isn't the first time I thought I was going to die. But… this time, I think it's gonna stick… You'll see what I mean.

If you'll hear me out, I'll explain everything in its place. I can't promise you anything as compensation—I don't have anything of value to bequeath to anyone. All I have left is my story. My legacy… It'll have to be enough.

You're my only hope of getting the truth to the world. You see, I have a confession… and a promise. I won't say whose, but there are hundreds of thousands of lives that depend on the truth getting out. Maybe even yours.

Because I have a secret. A secret I'm leaving for you, whoever you are. And the soul of a massive megalopolis hangs in the balance.

No doubt, by the time you read this, the rumors of my death will have spread like wildfire. They're true. But there's something else you should know. *I've saved the city.*

What I'm about to tell you is the truth of my time as the city's savior. Please—*Please*! My final request is that you help me set the record straight. Things cannot ever be allowed to get as bad as they did. It took me dying to fix them. You'll have to finish plugging the holes yourself. I just hope… but that's getting ahead of myself.

As they say, *everything in its place*. It's better that I start at the beginning. Before I got my wings… If I sound reluctant, it's because this wasn't one of my proudest moments.

Chapter One

The year was 2114. Old America. Jakob McCorbin was just elected President. Spring had finally started to fade and Summer was at our doorstep. The cars were still powered by the old steam & solar hybrid tech. Eternal Plasma Drives hadn't been invented yet. Railways had just made a big comeback for cross-country travel. I remember sitting under an advertisement for the Atlas Air&Ground commercial cross-country liner. Jerry and I would look up at that billboard and promise each other that when we got rich with our law firm, we'd book a car all the way out of Briar City, past HollyTown, past DoggWood, and all the way out of this continent!

Those were the days…

Let's see… 2114… The international crime was dropping all across the globe. We'd just come out of a big war against El Salvador. Jobs were at an all-time high. The politicians called it a utopia.

But those of us who lived in the ghetto thought it was another ordinary day in the history books. From our perspective, things didn't look so cheery. Jobs down there were still hard when you had them, and impossible to find when you didn't. Drug dealers still sold their products to school children. Gangs still put kids in caskets… they put a lot of kids in caskets.

That's why I, Sam Farsight, thought it would be a good idea to start a gang war.

The plan was simple. Goad the two gangs in Briar city, the SmashStones and the BloodBlades, into attacking each other and force the cops to *actually do something* to end them both once and for all.

Nothing is ever simple. I was about to find that out the hard way.

To find the SmashStone gang and learn their plans, I had to join them. A tricky feat since I lived in BloodBlade territory. If the BloodBlades ever found out I was with SmashStone, they'd kill me. Of course, if *either* of them found out what my real plan was, they'd both kill me anyway.

I thought I was so damn *smart* back then.

That was the year I turned twenty-one. It was the year I got a casket for a birthday present. Jerry, my best friend since grade school, found himself on the wrong end of a shooting.

That's where the Wingman found his start. Newly adulted. Chip on my shoulder. And the weight of the world in my back pocket. I wanted to do something with my life. But I decided then and there being a lawyer wasn't good enough for me. I wanted to do something "important."

God, I was so *stupid*. I even thought the city would erect a statue in my honor. I can't believe I was ever that dumb. The only thought on my mind was *no more kids in caskets*. I was going to end the gang wars forever.

That's why I was sitting on a brick wall in the rain across the road from the 14th precinct. One black kid against the world. That's why, when the cold wind blew across my face, I didn't back down. I was shivering and hungry and… and…

…

Lonely…

Yeah. That's the truth of it. I was so very lonely. I had a hole in my heart that was colder than the rain, and more painful than my stomach. That emptiness kept me moving. If I stopped… it would consume me.

I wasn't ever going to back down. Not until I did what I came here to do.

I checked my watch. 7:48 pm. He wasn't going to show tonight. I had to be back home before 9 o'clock or somebody would get suspicious. If not my family, then the gang. At the same time, sitting around in the rain waiting for a cop who might not even show wasn't the brightest idea I'd ever had. But the SmashStone goon I'd met with needed me to steal a cop car. And I had the perfect cop for the job.

Officer Filbert Warren.

A cop so dirty, garbage washes *him* off. The man's a walking personification of the seven deadly sins. But… If you looked past all that. If you ignored the stink, the stains, the empty burger wrappers he leaves instead of footprints. If you looked into his *soul*. You'd find a second, *even meaner* cop living in his gullet that just wants the world to burn.

Seriously! None of the other cops trusted him either. He earned himself the nickname "The Rat" back when he first joined the force, and he's done nothing but live up to his nickname since then. Rumor has it he's on *both* gang's payrolls. Witnesses against the gangs have a bad habit of going missing after this guy gets a look at their file.

Nothing's ever proven, of course. Rumors go on to say that IA has a file on him the size of Texas, but it's all full of dead ends, missing evidence, and hearsay. Which would be surprising because Officer Warren isn't smart enough to pull any of that off.

For example. Just as I was giving up hope that the fat rat masquerading as a cop would show up, he did.

The cop car slinked up to the front of the precinct like a pissed-off cat. The headlights glaring angrily ahead.

"Alright Berny, take this one in," I heard him say from across the road as he rolled down his window to throw out a sandwich wrapper. Littering is against the law. But Officer Warren didn't seem to mind as he dug into his burger with gusto.

Berny glared at his partner in disgust but said nothing. He went around and marched some kid into the building. The girl spat at him, but the weary patrolman didn't so much as flinch as he did his job. Apparently, he'd faced worse today.

Warren chuckled after they'd gone. He gulped down the rest of his burger in one bite and waddled out after them in leisure.

I swear the car rose two feet when he got out of it.

The fat lard even left the engine running. It was like he was begging for someone to steal it, but I hesitated. Not because I was having second thoughts. No, I hesitated because I knew I'd have to take a bath in acid after I'd sat anywhere Officer Warren had been. I could only hope the rain would offer me some protection.

I didn't waste time driving around once I was in the car. Sure, I stamped the pedal as far down as it would go, flashed the lights, and turned on the siren. I may have held my middle finger out the window like a good little delinquent, but I had a plan. The initiation required me to make some noise so people would know what I'd done, but I had to get away without getting caught.

I drove the car as fast as I could to the graveyard just past the hill on the edge of the city. I expected there to at least be some kind of chase, but apparently, Warren's fellow cops didn't put too much priority on his misfortunes.

I parked the car with the headlights flooding a row of gravestones. People who'd been killed by the gangs. I hoped it might remind *someone* they had a duty to fulfill. I opened the door and took off, being careful not to go around the front or the back where the cameras were.

Step one completed. Easy.

I should've known it was too easy.

Chapter Two

The next day, I skipped school. What did it matter to me? I was failing Biology101 anyway. It takes money to get an education. Money my mama should've been spending on the baby.

Instead of taking the bus uptown, I turned south and walked deeper into the Heap. That's the name we locals gave to the badlands. Cops won't protect you in the Heap. Every few years some hotshot fresh from the academy will take up a beat in the Heap to put the gangs on their toes. They never last long.

Down here your only choice is to aid the gangs or move away. Good luck trying to move away.

If you've never been to the Heap, it's not pleasant. Old brick buildings lean precariously against newer "affordable" housing projects. Cardboard replaced every other window. They held the whole place together with rusty nails and duct tape.

But what gets me is the smell. Imagine the contents of a million porta-potties after the annual chili festival all poured into a vat of booze and spilled across every sidewalk, every door, every lamppost, and every store. It's an all-out assault on your orifices. We call it *the Heap's welcome.* Newbies to the Heap never fail to toss their cookies, adding to its lustrous aroma.

Don't ask me how I could stand it. I grew up with that smell. To me, it smelled like home.

I walked quickly through BloodBlade turf. I tried to tell myself to calm down, but my heart wouldn't listen. *It's alright,* I told myself, knowing full well that talking to yourself is a sign of delusions. *No one knows you jumped in with the SmashStones yet.* Everyone on the block knew me. I saw old man Yin setting up his stir-fry shop. He waved like everything was normal. Did he know I was skipping school? Or did he just forget what day of the week it was?

Or, a darker part of me asked, *does he* know *you've joined the SmashStones, and he's just trying to keep you calm so you'll walk deeper into BloodBlade territory?*

Paranoia's a bitch.

I'd walked this street a bajillion times, never caring who's turf I was on. This was the first time I'd walked down it after Jerry died. I'd never appreciated how long the road was. Or how shady the buildings were. Or how many punks hid in the old places like cockroaches.

You wouldn't notice where BloodBlade turf became SmashStone territory. It's not like there's a line drawn on the ground. But I knew when I'd crossed it. I wasn't worried so much about getting shot as I was about the mission ahead of me.

Once more I thought about my mama. She's a kind person. She'd never hurt a fly if she could help it. Even now, twenty years after I'd seen her last, I have trouble remembering what she looks like. But I never forgot that smile. It was the kind of smile that cared about everyone. She would never have approved of this plan.

You're probably wondering why I didn't just pack it up and go home. So what if I stole a cop car? No one knew it was me. The gangs would assume I had cold feet—they get people like that every weekend. I could've left. I could've turned around, bought a meal off of Yin, and walked into Bio101 in just enough time to look like I was trying to be cool. I wish I could tell you that's exactly what I did.

But I didn't.

Instead, I turned off the main road and started walking in the narrow lanes between the buildings.

The idea of leaving haunted me every step I took… but I didn't… I never…

…

…

A part of me knew—even then—that it was already too late for me. I felt drawn down the path. An instinct that pulled me straight into the deepest danger.

I told you before; I was afraid of heights. But that never stopped me from climbing trees. In Briar City, we keep our State-mandated parks at the top of our skyscrapers. There's not a view like it anywhere else in the world. When I was a child, we'd dare each other to climb up on the rails and hang with our toes off the edge. Parents would freak out if they caught us—that's what made it fun!

When the others dared me, I would climb past the guardrail, up onto the concrete itself. I would stand up. And look down. Every time. I'd stare down the side of the building, wind brushing around me, and I'd think about falling. My heart pumped wildly, my feet would fill with lead. My mouth dried up.

It was like my worst fear was calling for me.

It was that same instinct that called to me walking down that alleyway. I couldn't have stopped even if I'd wanted to.

In front of me, the path opened up into a dead-end ally. At the end, a tacky pink bar sign hung over a ramshackle brick building. The lights had long ago been shattered. The Rock. Apparently, SmashStone couldn't resist the irony. It was one of those places that would've looked old even when it was new. SmashStone moving into the old karaoke bar didn't do it any favors. Vagrants slept on garbage bags stacked on the sidewalk. It baffled me to think that a trash truck could weave its way through the narrow paths that fed into this place. But then again, the trash was piled high enough… maybe they never did.

The smell of vomit was stronger here. But it wasn't the only scent in the area. The air was thick with a haze of marijuana and a twang of cocaine. The SmashStones were known for their drug addictions.

Presentation is everything. I walked through the door with little regard for who saw me enter. I stood up straight, as if I had all the right in the world to be in this dump. Not that it made much of a difference. For one thing, most of the "patrons" were lying everywhere unconscious from their long night of partying.

For another thing, I'm not actually all that tall. It's hard to look imposing when you're four-foot-nine.

It was a sickening place. Everything looked broken and dirty. The floor looked like it hadn't been cleaned in a decade. It stank of BO, and the air was heavy and thick from all the smoke. It made me choke. I knew coming here was a bad idea, but instead of leaving, I looked around the room and saw things I wish I hadn't. Gang members in various states of undress were strewn around the room. They'd partied until they dropped where they stood. Some of whom were in the middle of having sex.

With a sharp pain, I recognized one woman as a girl I had a crush on in high school. Seeing her lying naked on some thug tore me up inside in a way I still can't fully explain. She had a big contented smile on her face, and I remember being so haunted by it. I couldn't fathom how anyone could *enjoy* that kind of life. I would've given anything to unsee her sleeping there on him.

The sound of rough thumps and pained grunts disturbed my thoughts. It sounded like someone was getting beat up. It didn't take a genius to figure out that it came from the back room.

I was less confident walking past the sleeping crew. Before, I'd met Terry Mac, the recruiter, *outside* The Rock. I couldn't shake the feeling that I was going deeper into the devil's den.

Hand on the door, I pushed it open with as much bluster as I could manage. This time there was at least an audience.

"Sammy, Sammy, Sammy," the figure at the other end chided.

It was pitch-black in the room. The dusty light behind me revealed only a muscle-bound man in a green wife-beater, his back turned to me. Terry Mac. I heard a few more thuds and the clank of chains. It was a punching bag, not a body. I released a breath I didn't know I was holding.

"He-he. I heard about your little adventure last night," he said, stepping away from the bag and taking off his gloves. His hands were still wrapped in white gauze, but that didn't stop him from lighting a cigar. He puffed a rancid blast right at my face, causing me to cough. "The Rat squeaked quickly enough. You owe me a *thank you*. If I hadn't warned him about your initiation, you'd be behind bars." He looked over my shoulder and seemed to rethink his statement. "Well, behind *iron* bars," he chuckled at his own pun.

"Thank you," I said through gritted teeth.

"He-he-he," Terry Mac cackled. He took another long puff from his cigar—and then knocked me to the floor!

I didn't have time to react; the man lashed out faster than I could even see. *And I was looking right at him*. The door flipped shut, it's tiny plastic windows not enough to pierce the darkness. I fell to the floor. Terry Mac kicked at me. I tried to cover my gut with my arms and legs, but he knew all those tricks. His silhouette, a black form against the single ray of light from the door, leaned forward. A flurry of punches hit my sides. Something cracked. The dull red end of his cigar was the only thing that stood out.

I instinctively curled up into a ball and planted both feet as high as I could reach. I heard an "oof," but the red light didn't fall. A grip of iron clamped down on my calves and the next thing I knew I was being hurtled into the punching bag.

"Not bad, pebble," he said.

Getting back on my feet was no picnic. I felt like lead had been poured into my body. Except for my chest. The ripping, stabbing pain felt like someone had left a hot knife just under the skin. Standing up tall caused the room to sway like a boat on the water.

"Why did you come here?" he asked. All I could see of him was that damned cigar tip. It moved briefly as he flicked the ashes off the tip.

"I-I want to join you guys," I croaked out.

"I don't think so," Terry Mac retorted, giving me a swift box on the ears. The ringing was *unbearable*, but, as loud as it was, Terry Mac was louder still. "We had the Rat dig up everything about you for one of his *special* files. Your old man had a death sentence on him, your ma refused to pay the taxes. You've always been a good little boy, toeing the line and condemning our clients. Says here you even joined the college." He threw the file on the floor into the square patch of light. It lay opened with my picture pinned to several pages of thick text.

A full police file with all my personal information. The Rat had a busy night.

"I want revenge!" I shouted. Spittle and blood flew out of my mouth and landed splat in the middle of the file. I surprised myself. The truth just leaped out of me without any kind of planning, but already I could see how to spin it.

"My friend, Jerry was killed last week in a BloodBlade raid. I want them to suffer!"

"So you thought you could just join up with the SmashStones and kick them all into the dust," Terry Mac finished.

I nodded reluctantly.

"Grow up," the bruiser condemned. "You don't just decide to join up with us on a whim. That's not how it works. We only take people we can trust. For that, you've got to do us… a *favor*."

I hesitated. Terry Mac could see it. He flicked his ashes away irritably. "What kind of favor?"

Terry Mac's shadow loomed over me. I'd never felt so small before. My head throbbed; the pain was nearly unbearable. I thought longingly about my seat in Bio101. I'd never been so enthused to have the chance to fail a class again.

"It says here you live in BloodBlade turf," he said, gesturing to the blood-splattered file. "Last week they stole our biggest shipment of drugs. That's the attack that your *friend* got caught up in. If you want to join us, first you have to prove your loyalty by finding that shipment—and returning alive, of course. If you do that, you'll be one of us."

I couldn't believe my luck.

I laughed. Hard. Hard enough that I spit up more blood. I howled to the empty rafters above, dribbling my own blood down my chin like a madman.

Terry Mac took a step away from me.

"W-what's so funny!" He snarled, flicking his ashes away.

"You think I came here empty-handed? *I already know where the drugs are being held.*" I felt strangely light-headed despite the pain. Looking back, that was probably a warning sign of something unhealthy.

Terry Mac looked lost for words. "Where—How?!?"

"My cousin, Beck. He runs with the BloodBlades. He let it slip that he's on guard duty for their drug stash. Warehouse 15 near the docks. Even better. He let slip that one of their boys got busted yesterday, meaning they don't have enough manpower to guard the shipment around the clock."

Terry Mac was silent for a long time. When he spoke again, it was with bated breath. "When?"

I allowed myself to grin. "Tonight at nine o'clock. But you boys had better strike now. Because they move the whole shipment to a new location at ten."

I pushed a little too hard. Mac shook his head in disbelief. "That's too perfect!" He growled. He stepped in like he was going to hit me again. Instead of flinching, I stood taller; inviting him to hit me.

He hesitated.

"You just said I couldn't do this without *conviction*," I reminded him. "Look at me now. Do I look like I'm still doing this on a whim?" I couldn't see Mac. I couldn't look into his eyes. But I could *feel* the doubt radiating off him.

Terry Mac stepped into the square of light. He stared at the rafters in contemplation. It looked like he was having a silent conversation with himself. "Why should we trust you?" He said, at last, making eye contact.

I held his gaze; I *wanted* him to see my conviction. It would make it all the sweeter when I burned this bar to the ground. "There's only one thing on my mind," I told him truthfully.

"And that is?"

"I want Cutter to die."

A laugh cut through the darkness. Terry Mac withdrew against the wall. It was a deep, booming laugh that filled me with dread. There was only one person in the Heap who had a laugh like that.

A gigantic mass dropped from the rafters. The entire building shook at his landing. Terry Mac flipped an old iron switch, and the lights flooded the room.

"I like you, kid," the mass boomed. He was a veritable wall of muscle. The veins popped out against his skin, blue on red. His square face had slash marks crisscrossing all areas in a patchwork of scars. His wide grin revealed a mouth full of chipped teeth. The only white man in the entire gang. The infamous SmashStone.

A giant of a man, SmashStone easily stood seven feet tall. I couldn't tell you if my knees were shaking from the beating I just suffered or from this man's sheer *presence*.

He put his hand on my shoulder and it was like someone dropped a sack of cement on my back. I started to fall to the floor, but the behemoth's grip refused to let me collapse even as my knees gave out altogether. "It's not often I'll let in some unknown mineral off the street, but you've got *stones* in those britches, boy."

Honestly, I'm not sure what I said in response to this. Probably something like "hub-ub blek," since I was about two-thirds passed out already.

What I *do* remember is SmashStone grabbing the cigar right out of Terry Mac's mouth and planting the burning end right in the center of my chest. To say *it burned* would be a bit of an understatement. A drill burrowed its way into my chest! Charred skin and fried hair mixed with those noxious cigar fumes and ate their way up my nose. I howled to the sky, spitting up blood that would drip down my chest and mix into the inhuman concoction.

"Welcome to the SmashStones," he said. I fell to the floor and passed out.

Chapter Three

When I woke up, it was thirty minutes past noon. SmashStone and his thugs were gone. And so was my wallet. Terry Mac left a note on my face that read, *be at the east side of Warehouse 15 by eight-thirty or you're a dead man.* At least, I *assumed* it was Terry Mac who wrote it since I didn't think anyone else in the entire gang was capable of writing. *Except you,* a lingering sense of guilt reminded me.

The cigar hole in my chest still burned. My chest throbbed along dully until I tried to take a breath. It caught halfway and red-hot knives cut into my esophagus. I needed to go to a hospital… But there'd be *no way* a hospital would let me just walk out in a couple of hours… Besides… I… I wasn't finished being an *absolute* total dumbass yet…

I still had to talk with the BloodBlades.

This part of the plan was *much* less thought out than everything that's come before it… Somehow…

I had to make it into BloodBlade territory, find someone who wouldn't just shoot me at the first sign of my new "tattoo," and convince them to get to Warehouse 15 at the same time as the SmashStones…

The walk out of The Rock and back into BloodBlade turf gave me plenty of time to realize just how totally *whiffed* I was. Could I have still gone to the police? Yes. Did I?

If you thought the answer to that even *might* be 'yes,' you underestimate just how damned stubborn I can be.

No more kids in caskets, I told myself. *No more kids in caskets*. Every step felt like my bones were filled with lead. *No more kids in caskets*. Jerry's face at the visitation, so pale and porcelain. It was profane! *No more kids in caskets*. Did I have brain trauma? I passed Old Man Yin at his noodle shop. He looked at me like I was a nightmare. Dried blood running down my sides. No doubt he thought I'd been mugged… *No more kids in caskets, no more kids in caskets*! The BloodBlade hideout was plain as day. An old gym that closed down long ago. Was I really going to just walk in there? The thugs by the door just stood there in shock as I marched past them. *NO MORE KIDS IN CASKETS!*

"I demand to speak with Cutter!" I roared at the building. There were three fighting mats all lined up with people in and around them. My shout stopped them all in their tracks. I always did have a strong voice. Everybody in the room could see the hole in my chest, and no doubt every single one of them knew what it meant.

"The only way you're getting to see Cutter is an execution," a girl jeered from the side.

"You're not going to live that long!" another thug exclaimed.

Someone pinned my arms from behind, while a dude with long silver hair came at me with a knife. In case you couldn't tell, BloodBlades *love* their knives.

"Oh wow," you might be thinking, *"This must be how you died the first time."* Nope! That's still yet to come! No, this time around I managed to jump back against the guy who had my arms and kick the guy with the knife with all my might. I immediately dropped to the floor and lay there like a worm, too busy bleeding to death to really take note of the chaos that was exploding around me. Fun Fact: doing just about anything while one of your ribs is broken makes *everything* 100x's worse! Fighting for your life? Don't try that at home, kiddos.

The silver-haired guy pulled me up by what was left of my T-shirt and shouted… something at me. My vision was also getting kinda blurry. Whatever he asked, my witty response was to bleed on him.

Oh, yeah. Who's got the makings of a vigilante superhero? *This guy*.

Another guy dressed in grey sweatpants and a hoodie showed up and garbled something at Silver Hair. Next thing I knew, I was being dragged backwards through the gym while the others gawked at my broken body.

Side note, what is it with bad guys and dark rooms? Seriously! Don't they know torture rooms are *completely* unreliable? At best they were just putting me in a place where no one would hear my screa—on second thought everything checks out now…

The big guy tied my arms behind a chair and bound my legs for good measure. I tried not to panic.

Unlike the backroom at The Rock, this place had a proper ceiling over my head and charcoal grey drywall all around, so I didn't have to worry about Cutter just dropping in from above. But then again, I didn't get a good look at the room, so the iron door in front of me might not have been the only way in or out… but then *again*, again, if it wasn't the only way in or out of the room, why make the door out of iron?

I overthink pointless things like that. If I'd spent half as much effort thinking about my plan as I did about that small room, I wouldn't be in this mess in the first place.

After a brief spell, the guy who stopped Silver Hair from gutting me returned to the room.

Tying me up so I couldn't move and then putting me alone in a room for a few minutes was, honestly, the best thing they could've done for me. Sure, they could've *also* left a hot girl in the room to nurse my wounds and make sure I had plenty of water, but this wasn't too bad all things considered.

My head had cleared up a little. The world wasn't black and red anymore, and I was able to hear when the door opened. My body was still screaming pain signals to my brain, yes. But I wasn't about to pass out.

"You've got a lot of guts coming here alone," the man said.

"Unfortunately, I seemed to have left half of them back on 21st Street," I joked weakly.

A swift smack to the face showed just how much they cared for humor in the BloodBlade gang.

"Do you even know who I am?" he glowered.

Everybody and their cousin knew what Cutter and SmashStone looked like. Those two had been running wild down in the Heap for years. This guy wasn't Cutter. But he clearly had some authority to keep ol' Silver Hair from giving me a chest piercing. That could only mean the man before me was the vice-leader of the BloodBlades.

"Friday."

The man shook his head. "No. You should be thankful I'm not. Friday is Cutter's personal hitman. You'd already be dead in the ground if I was."

"Oh."

"I'm Seth Bridgess," he said as if it meant something.

I vaguely remembered a news report about Seth Bridgess, but I couldn't pin it down… until I could.

"Wait, you're just Cutter's drug pusher—" Bridgess stepped forward, his knife appearing in his hand like magic. "I-I mean—you're his *drug kingpin.* Ha-ha, yeah. Big guy, Seth Bridgess. The biggest drug dealer in the town."

Bridgess looked like I'd kicked him in the groin. Figures…

"That's right," he spit. "Drug kingpin… That's all I am… That murder-hobo Friday would've killed you on the spot, Do you care to guess why I left you alive?" This guy clearly had something going on behind the scenes…

… But… I saw an opportunity to lie some more.

"It's because of the second shipment," I said as casually as I possibly could.

Seth's face was *priceless.* "What second shipment?" *Hook, Line, and Sinker.*

I embraced as much of my inner coward as I could. It wasn't that hard; I had a lot of terror built up throughout today. "Oh, uh. O-of course not, you're k-keeping me alive because of… w-why exactly are you keeping me alive?"

"*What second shipment?*" Bridgess asked again, putting his knife to my throat for dramatic effect. It's a common misbelief that when someone holds a knife to your throat, you can feel the knife against your skin. I didn't. What I felt was a drop of warm, itchy wetness that ran down my neck.

"I have conditions."

The knife at my throat twitched. It was an infinitesimal movement, but enough to draw more blood. I felt pain now. A line of warmth at my Adam's apple that burned more the longer I waited.

"I want to be the one who kills SmashStone," I growled.

As I expected, Seth pulled his knife away. Bad guys are funny like that. Beg for your life and they'll just laugh as they kill you, even if it hurts them too. Tell them you want to kill their greatest rival? They'll give you a frickin weapon and let you walk out the door with it. As far as they're concerned, it's still a death sentence.

Bridgess peered at me suspiciously. What I said wasn't a lie *per se*. He could see it. But he was sharper than the usual thug. He had to be.

"SmashStone and his damned bricks are destroying this city," I claimed wildly. "I hate them! If they weren't tearing up the city, you lot wouldn't have had to steal from them—Jerry wouldn't be dead!"

"I get it," Bridgess snorted. "You're just a brat out on a revenge scheme. We get boys like you every other weekend."

I let go of another breath I didn't know I was holding. I tried to speak up again, but Bridgess cut me off with a furious look.

"But no one. I repeat, *no one* walks in here with a SmashStone burn on their chest and leaves unscratched."

"But I hav—"

"NO ONE chooses BloodBlades as a *second* choice! You're playing with fire and now you're going to get burned. Twice."

"I joined the SmashStones to find out where the second shipment was!" Seeing as how Bridgess didn't just skewer me on the spot, I took that as permission to continue. "It's high-grade Rock, like the first shipment. SmashStone always keeps half of the drugs that come through."

"Because he's a *user*," Bridgess interrupted. Everyone knew SmashStone was addicted to Rock; it's what caused his body to mutate so aggressively.

"Right," I said, thinking quickly, "But he had some left over from the last shipment." It was a shallow excuse, but it was one Bridgess bought. He twisted the knife in his hand anxiously. Like he wasn't sure if he wanted to stab me with it, use it to cut my bonds, or stab himself. Now that I had a train of thought, the rest of the story came easily. "He has enough left over to feed his habit this month too. But it's bad. SmashStone's pissed! He wants to retaliate for the raid even more than he wants the money from this shipment."

"That's preposterous!" Bridgess spat. I was impressed. I hadn't thought he'd know the meaning of the word, let alone correctly use it in a sentence.

"It's true! He's giving the whole shipment over to his boys tonight at ten. They'll be marching here to pull this building down brick by brick before eleven."

Bridgess punched the drywall. His hand tore right through it. "Over my dead body."

"Probably," I noted. Bridgess glared murderously. "I mean, probably—if I didn't know *exactly* where the second shipment was and when it was unguarded."

"Unguarded? How? Where?"

Hook, line, and sinker, I thought again.

Out loud I said, "Warehouse 15. You guys have caused more damage to them than you might think. Half their boys are out of commission and they've been forced to only post one guard during daylight hours."

"How—"

I cut *him* off for once. "I'm the guy assigned from nine to ten. The last chance for you and your crew to really put the hurt on SmashStone."

Seth Bridgess looked like he'd found religion. He made a show of distrust, much like Terry Mac before him, but in Bridgess's case, it was just the motions. He was halfway out the door before he remembered that I was still tied down in the room.

He neatly flicked his wrist, and the knife was at my bonds. It was a casual move, one he obviously didn't plan on, because his hand jerked to a stop mere millimeters away from granting me my freedom. It was clear, even in the moment, that some part of him was conflicted.

This was a dangerous moment for me. Technically, Bridgess *had* everything he needed for the op. I wasn't necessary. But on the other hand, if things went wrong, and I wasn't alive to take the blame, Cutter might just *shift* that blame.

"If I don't show up to my shift—*on time*—at nine o'clock the SmashStones will know something's up."

Bridgess hesitated. Whatever train of thought he had was shaken. "That's not enough." His breath washed over me, stinking of cigarettes—and something else. At the time I couldn't place that something. But it was a scent I would soon become intimately familiar with. I smelled almonds on his breath.

"If I take this to Cutter, he'll cut *me.* I need something damn good to tell them before they'll trust you."

Just like before, I held the goon's gaze. It worked with Terry Mac, so I thought hard about Jerry. It hurt so much to think about my friend. The only white kid in my class. Out of all of us, he alone had a chance to make good on his promise to escape the Heap. The rest of us would need a miracle. I was *looking* right at the guy who probably led the raid on the SmashStone drug transfer. If hate were a flame, I had enough fire to burn Bridgess alive. *No more kids in caskets.*

"You have what you need," I told him. "There's only one thing on my mind. *I'm going to kill SmashStone.*"

Bridgess let his knife fly. My bonds came loose and I slumped in the chair. My arms were weak. I'd already lost so much blood. My breath was ragged. My lungs couldn't have hurt more if I'd gotten a faceful of fiberglass dust.

"Thanks," I grunted. "Take this-take this information straight to Cutter. You'll need everyone. Have everyone there on the west side of the warehouse by eight-thirty. When nine o'clock rolls around, it's all yours."

Bridgess bobbed his head several times. "One more thing, kid."

I started to ask what it was, but before I'd even opened my mouth, Seth Bridgess poked his knife into the burn on my chest and twisted. For the second time that day, I screamed bloody murder.

"The pain. You take that, and you walk outta here with it. And just remember, if you back out now, there's *much* worse we'll do to you before we kill you."

I don't think I answered him. He shoved me through the door where I stumbled and fell. The other members jeered and threw red Solo Orbs at me. The Orbs are just some kind of mouth-sized seaweed compound that replaced plastic cups after the Great Corporate War. The company died along with the rest of them, but their name stuck around for some reason. Anyway, the Orbs didn't hurt too bad when they hit, but they did burst open like water balloons and drench me in various sports drinks.

I made it past the goons. The daylight struck at my eyes like a lance. My eyes burned even as I blinked about a million times to try and get them to adjust.

"Good luck kid," one of the guards murmured as I passed him. I couldn't tell you who it was, I never found out. As out of it as I was, I couldn't even tell you what the guy looked like.

I'd been through hell. There was only one place I wanted to go now. Home. And, fortunately for me, the place would be empty.

Chapter Four

Beaten, bruised, and broken. Oh yeah, today was going *exactly* according to plan…

I made it through the front door of our apartment and immediately stumbled towards my bed. The alarm clock next to the bed read 1:48 in bright, red numerals. Good thing I wasn't failing Math. I did a few mental calculations: I had to be at the warehouse by 8:30, which meant I'd have to leave the house by 7:00 at the latest. That left five hours to sleep and set the third part of my plan in motion.

The agonizing pain in my lungs reminded me that five hours wasn't nearly enough time to recuperate. Stupid lungs. They should know better than that by now.

As I approached the bed, everything went dark. I could vaguely feel myself collapsing, in a numb, underwater sense. I was well past my breaking point, but this was different. My mind was still running at top speed, even though my body was failing. The last time I blacked out, it happened too quickly for me to process what was happening. This time I was aware enough to be afraid of it.

I woke up tied to a chair. On top of our apartment. With my back leaning over the precipice!

The sight of the street below filled me with adrenaline. The chair was only a centimeter from slipping off into the void. I panicked, throwing myself forward against the straps, completely disregarding my previous injuries in one desperate attempt to get back onto the roof.

But an orange, scaled hand grabbed the chair's back, stopping me from leaning any further. Then, to my utter horror, it pushed me backward, tilting my face up into the sky as my full weight was brought down on the chair's already precariously placed hind legs.

I thought he was a myth! But that hand was real. The sun setting behind him burned right in my eyes! He pushed my chair further and further back, despite my protests. My heart was trying to beat itself out of my chest. Wind tousled my hair while I screamed. Once again, I couldn't stop myself from looking down. The ground was so far away, the pedestrians below were like ants on a picnic table. My eyes were glued to the asphalt twenty stories straight down.

With a herculean effort, I forced myself to look back at the *thing* in front of me. Burnished orange scales broke up his silhouette. Humanoid, but not human. His head—Oh God! There was nothing human about that head. Bulged over with a massive lower jaw. And at the top. Two glowing crimson eyes. It was like staring into the depths of Hell and seeing that Hell was staring back!

Movement behind him drew my attention to his tail. It twitched aggressively. "What do you know about Warehouse 15!" he growled. His voice! Even now, sitting alone in my cell, I shiver just remembering it. It was a low growl, impossibly loud! It was the voice of a dragon.

This was DinoHyde.

"Don't kill me!" I pleaded.

"Wrong answer!" he roared in return. With one hand—*one*—he pushed the chair all the way over the edge. I thought for sure I was about to fall. But the monstrosity still had hold of the back of the chair. Even as all four of the legs swung out into space, that grip held the chair in place. The straps cut into me. Slicing my already bruised body with every shudder.

"Y-you won't kill me—You *can't* kill me! DinoHyde n-never kills people." At this point, I was pleading more to myself than to him. He pulled me up, just enough to force me closer to those wicked eyes.

"What do you think happens to those people who mysteriously disappear in this city?"

"They were killed by the gangs?"

DinoHyde didn't answer. He didn't need to. I'd heard the tales in the Heap. We all did. Stories that a wild dinosaur was cloned in a lab and exposed to human DNA. No one *really* believes it. We all grew up just after that lawless age where vigilantes took up arms to keep the peace. Most of us just assumed DinoHyde was just another vigilante dressed up in a spandex suit.

Those scales seemed real to me. Somehow, those eyes bored themselves into my skull and pulled out my greatest fear from the deepest recesses. Tears burned their way out of my eyes. Even my mantra was forgotten.

"What do you know about Warehouse 15!" he asked again.

"I-I don't know anything about Warehouse 15," I cried, expecting to fall at any second. "It's just an abandoned Barron Corp storage site. I needed to find a place the SmashStones and the BloodBlades could go wild without getting anyone else hurt! That's it, *I swear!*"

DinoHyde seemed taken aback. He blinked his eyes a couple of times, at any rate. "You're not working for Lawson?"

"Who?" The name struck a chord with me, but I couldn't place it. I certainly wasn't working for him, whoever he was.

DinoHyde seemed to sense the truth. More confirmation of his supernatural powers. "It's not important," he said. He paused for a minute, his head cocked unnaturally.

A breeze blew around me. For a moment, I actually thought he was going to drop me. But the moment passed and DinoHyde swung me around back onto the roof. I was stuck facing away from the mutant vigilante.

I craned my neck so hard I swear something popped, but I still didn't get a good look at him—he just stepped into my blindspot no matter what I did.

"You should be in school, kid," he said. His voice was still gravely, but much less harsh. He still didn't know what to make of me.

"I'm not going to school anymore. I'm not going ever again," I returned stubbornly. God, I was such a prick.

"You don't know what you're playing at."

"How can you say that? We're on the same side!"

DinoHyde growled, "You're not on *anyone's* side, kid!" His voice returned to that deep reverberating tone that scared me so much. "You've made enemies of everyone in the city what with the stupid stunts you just pulled! Stealing a cop car, joining the SmashStones, marching right on up into a BloodBlades stronghold—it's a wonder you haven't killed yourself already!"

At the mention of my *heroic* deeds, my injuries started throbbing again. In addition to the busted ribs and the hole in my chest, I also had bruises on my back that stung like acid; a tender, itchy line across my throat; a cramp in my left leg; and a collection of cuts on my arms and shoulders. "I guess I just don't have the talent for dying."

DinoHyde smacked at the back of my head lightly. My vision doubled as my eyes crossed from the pain. Add one concussion. Lovely.

"Give it up, brat. You don't have what it takes to make it in this line of work."

"*Screw you!*" I spat indignantly. "You know, i-if you were out *protecting* people instead of throwing kids off building tops, I wouldn't have to be here, a-and my friend would still be alive!"

You know, I didn't think I was doing anything particular by bringing the conversation around to Jerry again. It took me by surprise to realize I meant it this time. Seeing the myth right in front of me… Damn… That gave me someone to blame. Someone besides the gangs. After all the lies and half-truths… This was real. And it *hurt*.

I bawled for a solid minute. I've never been any good at handling grief. Even now it's easier to just escape into the past and forget the last couple of days… forget what's happening to me.

DinoHyde let me cry. He waited for me to calm down before he said, "I was sorry to hear about Jerry." That was it. No nonsense, or *he's in a better place now* like all the other adults kept repeating.

Just, sorry.

"He was a good kid," DinoHyde continued. "Smart. Honest. I wish I *could've* stopped what happened to him."

"THEN WHY DIDN'T YOU!" I shouted. "You're the monster vigilante! You're the one going around playing hero! Why didn't you—or any of the others—protect *him*!"

I expected him to smack me over the head again, or maybe tell me off for being a brat. I would've deserved either. But instead, DinoHyde just made an odd wheezing noise that I eventually recognized as a sigh. "It happened in the daylight. I can't operate so freely during the day."

"Whatever," I huffed. I could never accept such an easy answer. "As soon as you let me go I'm going to clean up your mess for good. There won't be any more kids in caskets."

"It's not that easy."

"Well, maybe you just haven't been *trying* hard enough!"

DinoHyde spun the chair around into the setting sun. He towered over me, those red eyes blazing. "Listen to me, kid! What you're doing won't work. The gangs aren't just going to kill each other off just because Sam Farsight has a grudge against them. All you're going to do is start a war that'll burn down this whole city."

I dug my toes into my shoes and forced myself to stare anywhere but at his eyes. The building next to us had a park on its roof. Empty, of course. Most buildings locked their roof access at sunset. It was—

"-Sunset…!"

"What are you going on about now?" DinoHyde asked.

"It's sunset! And none of the buildings near my apartment have a park on them! Where am I? What time is it??"

DinoHyde huffed. "Relax, kid. We're near the docks, and it's only 7:30-ish."

I quickly ran some more mental calculations. "There's still time, but I've got to hurry. Are you going to let me out of this chair?"

"I will. But I won't help you. What you're doing is suicidal. Both Cutter and SmashStone will be pissed. Even I can't take them both on at once."

"That's fine," I snapped. "I didn't want your help anyway."

"This isn't a game, brat!" DinoHyde growled again. (He does that a lot.) "If you go through with this they *will* kill you. And I won't be there to save you."

"Then I'll die!" There was something in the force of my shout that gave the vigilante pause. Conviction, plain and simple. I knew the dangers. But that wasn't going to stop me. "At least I'll die knowing it wasn't in vain. Knowing that I made a difference."

"Kid…" DinoHyde began. But he stopped. Making another one of his strange sighs, he reached behind me and unbuckled the straps that bound me. I wasn't going to stay and chat. I was already limping off to the door.

"Kid!" he tried again. "Listen to me—look, there's a better way. A proper way. Just back down from this madness and I'll—"

"I don't want your help! *I'm* doing this *my* way. I don't want anything to do with you!" I limped down the steps, all twenty flights of them. DinoHyde didn't follow after me. I don't know what he did after I left. I didn't care.

Was I reckless? Yes. Was I stupid? Yes. Do I regret my actions that day? Oh, most *definitely*. Did I care at the time? Nope… I was convinced I had things figured out. DinoHyde was just one more test of my resolve.

Chapter Five

First stop, the nearest phone booth. Dedicated land-lines really made a comeback in the public sector after computers took over all the airwaves. Best of all, they're free.

I angled my broken body into the phone booth, taking extra care to block the camera as I stepped in. I dialed 911.

"Please state the nature of your emergency," a robotic voice clicked.

"Witness to a crime," I said with as much of a falsetto as I could muster.

The robotic voice provided it's pre-recorded response. "Please give details while dispatch is notified."

I covered the receiver and coughed to clear my throat. The falsetto was hard on my voicebox. But I'd practiced the false voice for hours after the funeral. It was the only way I could fake the voice trace so it wouldn't lead the cops to my front doorstep.

"I just witnessed two very scary men enter Warehouse 15 with large guns across their backs. One of them mentioned a drug raid. I think they were gang members. One had a knife in his hand."

A few seconds after I'd stopped speaking the robotic voice spoke up again, "Thank you for your report. Your audio recording will be added to the file. You may be called to verify it before a court. Please speak your name and number now, or in case of emergency please wait on the line until an officer can be dispatched to your location."

I left the receiver on the dash and hobbled out of the booth as quickly as I could. The police were notorious for being quick to investigate a prank call, but slow to actually do something about real crime. My testimony would be enough for them to investigate Warehouse 15, but it would take them an hour to actually do something about it. With just a little luck, they'd walk in right at the same time as the two gangs.

This was my master plan. No doubt I'd be arrested too, but I was prepared for that possibility. I didn't really have much of a life to leave. I'd testify as quickly as I could, express every detail I witnessed, and confess the actions I'd done. I'd have to go into witness protection, maybe even serve time, possibly even be killed. But both gangs would be off the streets forever. No more kids in caskets ever again.

You couldn't get a better deal than that.

The east side of Warehouse 15 faced the ocean. Once upon a time, this place was a booming center of commerce. But those days had long passed. The road was riddled with more potholes than swiss cheese, and the wooden pier missed planks here and there in its path down to the open ocean. Old ships still docked along the rickety structure. Some even had lights on inside, but some had been dark for years.

The sun was setting over the water, turning it bright orange with a few shadows where the waves rippled. If it had been any other day, I would've stopped to watch the sunset. Today, I hobbled past it.

I had a problem. I had to keep the BloodBlades and the SmashStones away from one another until the police could arrive. The problem was I had no idea *how*. If I'm being honest, I never expected to get this far in the plan.

The SmashStones were holed up behind some crates on the pier. They all looked foaming at the mouth. A handful of *very* aggressive looking women from The Rock were scattered amongst the dudes. It only occurred to me at that moment that they were part of the gang too and not just some random hookers. Terry Mac noticed me immediately and gave me a glare that could halt a rampaging elephant.

"You better not have lied to us!" he hissed as soon as I got close enough.

"What's the problem?" I asked, trying so *very* hard to play it cool.

"*The problem*!" he started, the others hushed him anxiously giving the warehouse a suspicious glance. Terry Mac caught himself and lowered his voice. "The problem is this place is *empty*. No guards have walked by here at all the whole day. Lights are off, and the Rat tells us this place is owned by Barron Corp."

"This place *is* owned by Barron Corp," I said quickly. The other gangsters looked worried. One made the sign of the cross and muttered something under his breath. Only Terry Mac looked unphased by this.

"I'm surprised they have the stones," he glowered angrily. "They know the rumors about DinoHyde as well as anyone."

"Wait, what's this about DinoHyde?" I asked. "I—uh—I thought he was a myth."

One of the goons spoke up, "A Barron Corp scientist created him in a lab accident fifteen years ago. Laugh all you want, kid, but *something* beats the shit out of anyone who steps foot on Barron Corp property without permission."

"But this place has been abandoned for *ages*." Terry Mac reasoned. "The BloodBlades musta' figured out he don't stop here anymore. Otherwise, they wouldn't have stashed our rock here."

"Exactly!" I said, hopping on the convenient excuse. "As for the guard, he's inside. I—uh—walked by the west side before coming around here. Took a peek through the window—"

"He didn't see you did he?" Terry Mac cut in.

"No! No. He was faced this way muttering something about calling in his shift after he left." I'd witnessed no such thing, of course. But the lies came easily enough now that I'd had practice. Anything that kept the SmashStones on *this* side of the warehouse saved my bacon. I had to time this *exactly* right. But without knowing when or where the cops would show up, it was a bit like walking down in the subway rails without a watch. If you've never tried it

before: *don't*!!

I couldn't put my finger on it, but something was nagging me about the

SmashStone gang. No time to think about it, I continued with my story.

"According to my cousin, this guy's set to leave at nine o'clock on the dot. But

his replacement can't be spared until ten. If we time this right we'll just walk in

there, grab the rock and be out before anyone from the BloodBlades even knows

something's up."

Terry Mac was impressed. "Good work, slab. You show initiative, that's

something a lot of our boys could learn from you." He made a pointed look to

one of the thugs in the back. A grungy man who wore layers of rags and had

shoes that were falling apart. He didn't answer. Instead, he averted his eyes and

muttered something too low to catch.

That's when it hit me. Our crew was only about twelve people, counting

me. "Where are all the others? Why isn't SmashStone here?" I asked Mac.

"Kid, do you honestly think SmashStone himself bothers with

something as trivial as stealing from the BloodBlades? No! He's back at The

Rock Bar getting high and tearing up."

"But… what if something goes horribly, horribly wrong?"

Terry Mac drew a long puff on his cigar before answering, spreading its noxious fumes everywhere. "If something goes wrong here, I get to hit you in the face and then SmashStone will smash *you*, rip you into pieces, and bury the pieces under enough concrete that no one will ever find the body."

I couldn't answer. A lump grew in my throat, helped along by the cigar fumes. Terry Mac tossed that threat out as casually as if he was talking about a trip to the beach. After all the abuse my body had gone through today, I believed him. SmashStone wasn't here. One way or another, my plan to stop the gangs had already failed… *DinoHyde was right.*

Terry Mac continued. "We've got hundreds an' hundreds of stones all throughout the city. Addicts, and dealers alike. We have kids in the schools, cops on the force, ordinary soccer moms in the suburbs—the works. SmashStone oversees all of that. He deals with the money, he makes the contacts, he orders us to tear things up. We obey and have a shit-ton of fun in the process."

His crew gave a hushed cheer, slugging each other on the arms.

"I'll bet SmashStone even has some stones running wild right now to keep the BloodBlades distracted."

If he had hit me in my chest again it wouldn't have hurt like his words did. Everything I did, every lie I'd said… It was for nothing—*nothing*! No doubt, the same could be said for the BloodBlades. I never even saw Cutter face-to-face. Or Friday, his right hand. Every break, stab, burn, bruise, and cut on my body throbbed. Reminding me of everything I went through to get here… Reminding me there was no way out. I was going to die. But I wasn't going to end the gangs. At best, I was going to lock up a few drug dealers.

It's not fair!

Terry Mac and the others could see my expression. Luckily for me, he had a different interpretation of what was going on in my head. "Look, kid, you did good here. Keep this up and Cutter's going to feel the hurt. And when he does, we're going to stab him with his own God-damned knife."

The others let out a muted cheer, keeping one eye on the warehouse. But me? I snapped. I did not come all this way so a *drug dealer* could lift my broken spirits! He deserved to die! They *all* deserved to die!! Forget the police, forget DinoHyde, forget Sam F-ing Farsight and his clever plans! They were all going to die. Tonight. The law be damned.

No more kids in caskets.

"That's the spirit kid," Terry Mac grinned, taking another long draw on his cigar. The smug bastard.

Already an idea was forming about how I was going to get the job done. I just had to wing it a little while longer.

"Anyone got the time?" I asked.

Terry checked his watch. "It's time," he grunted.

"I'll go first," I volunteered quickly. "Check and make sure that the guard has actually left."

"Take Martin with you," he said, pointing out the man in rags.

"Why me, boss?" the man complained.

"Because I'll smack you one if you don't, you lazy good-for-nothing."

I interrupted them, "If all's clear, I'll send him back to let you know. Wait ten minutes, and then we'll—uh—tear this building a new one."

"Why wait?" Martin asked. "You're not planning on stealing a share, are ya?"

"No! I just want to check something out." Everyone was glaring at me suspiciously so I added, "You're holding me responsible for this. I… I'm worried this might be a trap. That's all."

"You'd better pray it's not," Terry Mac confirmed, flicking his ashes at my face. "Here," he pulled out a gun and put it in my hands. "If this *is* a trap you've led us into, you've got ten minutes to make it right."

Chapter Six

I swear the gun weighed five pounds. I'd never held a gun before, but I didn't think they could be that heavy. Me and Martin slinked around the warehouse cautiously. I tried to mimic Martin's form, low to the ground and almost pressed against the building. His rags gave him an advantage. They were all dark textured; he nearly vanished in the shadows. I couldn't move like that. My every step echoed in his silence. Even my breath resounded no matter how softly I tried to breathe.

Of course, there was no reason to be silent. The BloodBlades should be holed up somewhere on the side facing the Heap. I doubted anyone would attack us. The BloodBlades wanted to make this operation as stealthy as possible. Meanwhile, Martin seemed to be the only SmashStone *capable* of stealth. I had the pieces, even back then. If I had time to think I might've figured out what was about to happen. But I didn't. And I didn't.

Martin signaled for me to stop. He held his gun straight up, clasped in both hands like they do in all the movies. I tried to mimic it, but my hands shook. Martin cocked his head unnaturally. His face was so wrapped up the movement was the only way I could tell he was looking at me questioningly. "Have you ever shot a gun before?" he asked

"O-of course I have!" I lied indignantly.

Martin looked at me in silence. I couldn't meet his gaze. "Your safety is still on," he said in a tone more sad than angry. "You're left-handed; grip your trigger hand *hard* with your right. It's your base. Keep your left hand relaxed except for the trigger finger. Keep the gun pointed away from you and…" He turned away. He slumped against the wall with a muted thump and looked up to the darkening sky.

"And?" I prompted, adjusting my grip and trying desperately not to forget the tips Martin just spouted off.

"Always aim at center mass," He said reluctantly, pointing at his chest in demonstration.

"I-I got it."

"You can still leave, you know?"

That took me by surprise. Martin was a SmashStone member. A junky, a thug. Was he testing me? I didn't know.

"I can't leave—I won't."

"No… I didn't think you would." I tried to read Martin's expression. Was it me, or did he sound… sad? He didn't sound like the other thugs in the gang. I started to question him, but the words choked in my throat. Martin turned away and gestured for me to follow. "Come on, let's finish this and go home."

I had no choice but to follow.

I found the BloodBlades almost immediately. Martin, so focused on the warehouse, didn't look around too much. I was the only one to see Bridgess poke his head out of another abandoned building on the other side of the warehouse. He had a hard, pinched look about him. He caught my eye seriously and gave a pointed glare before stepping back into the shadows.

"It's all clear," Martin said.

"What did you expect?"

He pointed at the gun in my still shaking hands. "What did *you* expect?"

I couldn't answer him. I couldn't even try to look him in the eye. Not that it would've done me any good to try. I'd never seen anyone wrapped in rags like a leper in all those documentaries. If the situation was different, I might've asked him about it. Looking back, I should've. Things would've turned out… *differently*.

At the time, I was more focused on trying to get him back to the SmashStones so I could continue with my plan… I…

It was easier not to think about him as a person. I knew, if I did that, it would just make things harder.

Before I continue, I want to clear up one thing. I don't think, having had twenty years to look back on this incident, that I *could've* killed anyone going into that warehouse. Let alone *would've*. As you'll see, I never got the chance to test that resolve… Considering how the rest of my life turned out, I think it's safe to say I wouldn't have been able to commit murder. But when you're young, you don't know what you don't know, and you think what you *do* know is all there is….

You—*I* was wrong. Obviously. But if you really want in my headspace, it was a really simple place. I was hurting, and I'd dived so far into this mess that I couldn't see any other way out of it.

So when Martin asked what I was expecting, that stung a bit. Martin seemed like a nice enough guy for a drug-addicted, gun-toting, gangster. He, at least, had a calming effect on me. Maybe it was just because he was the only person I'd met all day that hadn't tried to kill me… but I was planning to kill him… Those kinds of thoughts really mess with your head. And you don't even want to *know* what it does to your heart.

Martin apparently got bored of waiting for me to answer. Or maybe he just thought he'd scored a point on my ego, I really don't know. Either way, he holstered his gun and started back the way we came.

Ten minutes before all Hell broke loose. And only God knew how long it would take for the police to arrive.

Fun.

Bridgess was waiting for me with only ten men. Because *of course,* he was only waiting with ten men. *Drug raid, shrug maid.* Visually, the

BloodBlades weren't that much different from the SmashStones. Instead of a raggedy bunch of black and Hispanic thugs in wife beaters, they were a raggedy bunch of white thugs in wife beaters. It's like every thug in the city was allergic to proper clothes. I will say that, while the SmashStone dudes usually had pink or orange boxers showing out of their baggy pants, the BloodBlades seemed to prefer blue and green. Truly, this was valuable information worth nearly dying for.

I put on my nicest, calmest smile as I approached Bridgess. The second I walked through the door, all eyes jumped on me. No one was sitting, but I got the feeling if they had been, they would've jumped up as I approached Bridgess. It was impossible to keep a carefree smile while ten white guys glare bloody murder at you, so I stopped trying.

Seth Bridgess himself couldn't be read. His eyes seemed to stare right through me as he spoke up. "Was that the other guard."

"Yep. He's gone now."

Bridgess nodded. His mouth was drawn thin. Like *pencil-line* thin. I cocked my head reflexively, trying to figure out what was up with him when he pulled out a gun.

Everyone in the room started pulling out their guns and knives and aiming them right at my face.

"Whoa, whoa! Guys! We're all friends here," I tried.

Bridgess shook his head slowly. "Warehouse 15 is *Barron Corp* property. It's DinoHyde's territory. You, our little turncoat friend, are our bargaining chip. That mutant freak won't dare attack us while we have a hostage. So you're going to walk us in there. Nice and slow. If you run—if I think for even a *second* that you're about to betray us…" He cocked his gun dramatically. That action in itself made it all pretty clear to me. "You know, I did warn you" he continued. "I told you, no one *ever* chooses us BloodBlade's second… *and lives to tell about it.*"

"You should've stayed in your stinking bar," one of the guys sneered.

"No, even better," another called out. "He should've stayed in Africa with his kin!" There was hooting from all sides of the room.

One of the ones in the back shouted out. I'll leave it for you to guess which racial slur he called me.

I started for the bastard. I really did! If I had my way, I woulda clocked him back to the 1900s… But, unfortunately… here in the 2110s, the other BloodBlades cocked their guns eagerly. Bridgess alone didn't seem to care one way or another what happened to me. His gaze was focused off in the distance.

I tried to appeal to him. "You're *really* judging me on my skin color? I thought your lot didn't give a shit about that." Okay, so it wasn't one of my better appeals. But in fairness, I was pissed.

"Oh, most of us don't," Seth shrugged, still looking off into outer space. "But, you know. These guys are volunteers."

"Still, isn't it a bit… outdated? I mean you guys still have your pride to—"

He cut me off by hitting me on my nose. My eyes teared up and a fresh wave of blood ran down my face. "Do you know how I know this is a trap?" he said, drawing close to whisper in my ear. I shook my head *no*, but said nothing. This whole situation felt more *off* than normal. I didn't trust myself to speak.

"It's because you said we'd 'need everyone,' for a simple drug raid."

My eyes rolled *hard* as I groaned internally. It was like Terry Mac said. *Of course*, they wouldn't need everyone. Any *real* gangster would know that wasn't how the gangs operated.

"Now, move it!" Bridgess demanded, pushing me back the way I came. "We've got a shipment to rob."

Chapter Seven

How *whiffed* was I? … Oh… let me count the ways.

One. Not *a single part* of my plan came to fruition. Now instead of having a gang war take place with me hiding somewhere for the police to show up, I was smack-dab in the middle of it.

Two… None of the leaders were there. So this whole thing was pretty much a complete wash.

Three. The one *thing* that could help me, DinoHyde, was probably long gone by now. He swore he wouldn't stop me from getting killed, and I basically told him to shove off.

Four. Every single person gathered here at Wearhouse 15 had one common enemy… me.

It wasn't a long walk from where the BloodBlades were hiding and the warehouse. With each step, I thought of yet another reason I should've just stayed in school failing Bio101. This was the worst day of my entire life…

Well… *second* worst…

One thing for the warehouse: it was *big*. My descriptions outside didn't do it much justice. Inside was row after row of empty crates and spilled boxes, the rafters above creaking from the wind, the roof up so high it wasn't even visible in the twilight. This place would've been a sight to see in its heyday. With the broken forklifts running up, down, and all around, it would've been the poster child for trade and high-maintenance storage. Now, it was just a poster child for abandoned projects.

I didn't turn my head much, but from the corners of my eyes, I could see bright labels from companies that died off a long time ago during the Corporate War. Back then, vigilantes were honored heroes. They were a dime a dozen… what I wouldn't do to have one there with me at that moment.

I continued leading Bridgess and his cronies straight down the warehouse. No twists, no turns. Just right down the center path. I didn't want them to get lost. Or, more to the point, miss it when the SmashStones entered.

And what an entrance it was! One minute, nothing. The next, there was a groan that shook the whole building! In front of me, the double doors split apart, revealing the last vestiges of the sunset.

Terry Mac walked right down the center, the haze of his cigar causing the line of gangbangers following him to blur. "Now why," he drawled, his gun out and pointed straight at us, "am I not surprised by any of this?"

Unfortunately, I couldn't answer him. Seth Bridgess, at the first sign of trouble, grabbed me by the neck and put his gun to the side of my head.

"I was expecting the police," Bridgess called out. His boys quickly toppled over large boxes from the shelves on either side as cover. Behind him, Terry Mac's SmashStones did the same.

Terry Mac continued to take a few more steps towards Bridgess and myself, despite Bridgess gesturing wildly with the gun. "So," Terry asked. "What you say, pebble? How does it feel to be played by these goons? Sucks doesn't it? Next time, you'd better be damn sure about what you're getting the rest of us into before you go making promises."

"That's assuming he gets a next time," Bridgess sneered coldly. "You think this boy's still working for you? You're wrong, Mac. You're always betting on the wrong horse."

"That's the thing about you killers and your stupid knives. You just kill anyone that screws up. We hurt 'em. Teaches them so they don't do it ever again."

"Dead men don't make second mistakes."

"Dead men don't buy more product."

"Dead men don't steal product when they're out of cash."

While the two of them were having their showdown, the SmashStones I could see were picking their targets with frightening expertise. Bridgess' grip kept getting tighter and tighter. I tried to pull his arm away with my right hand. I couldn't breathe! My body was already at its limit. Bridgess, being nearly a whole head taller than me, was pulling me up off the ground. And he kept shifting. Hiding his sleazy face behind me so no one could get a shot in.

Behind me, I could hear guns swish and click as the BloodBlades shifted targets. The SmashStones in front were clearly more disciplined with guns. They were calm. But even then, the tension was showing. Sweat ran down one man's brow. A woman kept flexing her trigger finger at any sign of aggression.

It all came down to who shot first.

That's when Martin stepped forward. "Sorry folks!" He said in a deep, arrogant, and melodic tone that was completely at odds with his earlier attitude. "But I'm going to have to stop this before it gets completely out of hand."

Even I was caught off guard by his tone. And, judging by the fact no one else opened fire on him, I'm guessing everyone else felt the same way.

"What the hell do you mean by that?" Bridgess asked, gripping my neck even tighter.

"Martin! Now's not the time for your stupid quirks." Terry Mac scolded.

"Alas!" Martin resounded. "You don't seem to understand. I'm here for both of you!"

Before either of them could recover from their shock, I managed to get my left hand on the trigger of my gun. I remember seeing old television shows where goofballs accidentally shot themselves in the foot because their guns went off in their holsters. *And I had put away my gun without turning off the safety!* I angled the gun as far back as I could and pulled the trigger.

Bridgess let out a yelp like a dog, and I fell to the floor. Shots rang out overhead, flying from one gang to another. In front of me, Martin's raggedy shoes transformed.

In a flourish, he unraveled the raggs around his body and threw them across all the combatants. Terry Mac, being the closest, was caught in so many he fell to the floor too. Where Martin had been standing was now a tall, lithe man wearing a bright red bandit's mask and a green spandex suit.

"No way," I breathed.

The man moved gracefully. Leaping over the makeshift barricades and knocking over SmashStone thugs left and right, before leaping across the void to do the same against the BloodBlades. Miraculously, none of the bullets ever came close to him. He ducked and weaved around all the combatants like he was made of water. But his feet were made of steel! Where he kicked, people flew! And they didn't get back up.

This was the Runner, and in a span of six seconds he took out ten goons, five on each side.

No doubt he would've finished off the rest too, but the unthinkable happened.

From the side, a child's voice cried out. "Help me mister superhero! Help me!"

How did I not see him before? A little kid tucked away in between two shelves. Had he been there the whole time? How? Why??? -I… my brain shut down.

Bullets were still flying in every direction. I don't even think anyone was aiming anymore. Just firing in a blind panic. One bullet ricocheted off the shelf mere inches from the kid. This was my worst nightmare come true! That kid was going to end up in a casket… *and it was my fault.*

The Runner, seeing the kid, saved my soul. He danced his way near the boy, scooped him up in one fluid motion, and took off through the shelves!

The Gang members that were left didn't know what to do. Terry Mac wriggled his way free about the same time that Bridgess managed to crawl his way off the other side.

Terry Mac took off after him. I followed suit, while the gangbangers with any wits left reopened fire on each other.

Two shelves passed, but there was no sign of either of the lieutenants. My heart was trying to make its way out of my chest again. In the moment, I'd forgotten all about my pains again. I tore through the next shelf and heard a gunshot. Whipping around the last shelf I found Terry Mac standing over Bridgess.

"This one is for our missing shipment you sick son of a bitch," he pulled the trigger.

Seth Bridgess breathed no more.

I didn't even have time to contemplate what to do next when I was grabbed from behind yet again. I tried to escape, but this new guy was wise to every trick I tried. I couldn't even see him. But I did manage to kick the shelf in my struggle.

"Friday!" Terry Mac exclaimed. Before he could even draw his gun, there was a swish in the air and three knives appeared in both of Terry Mac's legs and his right arm. His pistol clattered away under the nearest shelf.

"Sorry, Mac," Friday said in a thick Chicago accent. "The boss wants to have a word with this one immediately—Now, now," He said, swiftly cutting off

Terry Mac's protests. "Just be thankful I'm after *his* head and not yours. You're allowed to live to get high another day. For now… But don't think I won't tell Cutter what you did to our boy Bridgess."

A mechanical bullhorn announced, "This is the police, you are surrounded. Surrender or we will open fire!"

I was getting really sick of being held like a helpless kitten. If I was going to die anyway, I wanted to try to free myself. But Friday was too strong. I made one last attempt to get free. Friday rewarded those efforts with another blow to the back of the head. I passed out.

Chapter Eight

I woke up in the darkness. Somebody was dragging me up a flight of stairs, head first. My groggy mind couldn't process what was happening. But when I tried to wipe the sleep from my eyes, I discovered my hands were tied together with duct tape.

And then I tried to scream and realized my mouth was gagged.

Friday laughed. His voice echoed in the small stairwell, coming from all directions. "None of that, kid. If you struggle too much, I'll start dragging you up feet first."

This wasn't my day.

Friday ambled along. Dragging me slowly up each step. My back was on fire! Each time we went up, the step would scrape my back, running a sharp pain all down my body.

I winced when one stopped right on one of the sores Terry Mac gave me earlier in the day. Friday laughed again. The monster was enjoying this.

We went up another few steps onto a landing. Friday kicked in the door and slung me around like a sack of potatoes. I bounced and then rolled a couple of times against the concrete.

Night had fallen completely. A storm must've rolled in because rain was falling. This building didn't have any guardrails. The concrete just vanished after a few feet from where I landed. A haze of light below the lip was the only thing that suggested civilization was still there.

"I hope you enjoy the view," a rough, gravelly voice spoke up from behind me. I'd heard that voice before. Everyone had. This voice once declared the entire city as his own. Every now and then the news would replay it. Children would crawl under their sheets in fear of it. "It says here you hate heights." A file slapped down in front of me. It was the file the Rat made for the SmashStones. The rumors were true, the Rat must've leaked to both sides.

"It was a clever game, kid," the infamous Cutter continued. "No, wait. That's not it at all. What's the opposite of clever?" He asked Friday rhetorically.

"Stupid."

"Yes, stupid…. Ignorant. Ideotic. Brainless. Mindless. Obtuse. Moronic. Inane… and even futile. The depths of this doltish, dopy, half-backed scheme of yours is so mindless, insensate and puerile that there aren't enough adjectives in the world to describe the depths of its pointless, naive creation!"

"That's sixteen, boss. A new record."

Cutter harrumphed impassively. "An irony. I wasn't even trying this time. A slip of the habit and nothing more."

Friday didn't respond.

Cutter kicked me in the back, forcing me nearer the precipice. "Put him on his feet," he commanded.

Friday walked into my vision. Black boots. Black socks. Black overcoat. Black belt. Black leather pants. Black shirt. Black broad-brimmed hat… I'm thinking the guy had a thing for black. He reached down with his black leather gloves and pulled me up by the duct tape around my wrists.

I was in no condition to stand. For one thing, my legs were bound in three places. For another, I was so thoroughly beaten and bruised the only thing that kept me upright was Friday.

Cutter walked in close. His face was porcelain smooth. Not a hair to be found on his aged features. And not a wrinkle. The man had to be at least seventy. But he didn't look a day over thirty. A fedora pulled low over his head, his yellow eyes caught what little light there was and echoed it back like a reflective lens. He also wore a big, black overcoat. But unlike Friday, who let his fly in the wind like a cloak, Cutter had his buttoned up tight.

"Bridgess was a good subordinate," Cutter said. "Loyal. Efficient. He did what he was told and buried the bodies without asking."

"He could hold his liquor pretty good too," Friday interrupted.

"Yes, that too. He was never drunkenly, and he never sampled his own product. He was valuable to me."

As if to punctuate how valuable, Cutter punched me in the gut. I spit up more blood… a new record… yay… It couldn't make its way past the gag, though, and leaked out the sides of my mouth. The only thing more disgusting was how much of that I ended up swallowing while trying to get my breath back.

Not. My. Day.

You might be wondering what was going through my head right now. The answer is, not much. I thought I was going to die.

And…

…

I welcomed it. I wasn't looking for any way to escape. I just wanted a way *out*. Preferably, a fast way.

Cutter drew out his knife. For a group of people called the "BloodBlades," you'd think the leader would carry some kind of grand blade. Jewel encrusted and blessed by the holy sages or something. But no. Cutter's blade was a simple straight razor. But in Cutter's hands, that knife transcended its humble creation.

Cutter's eyes lit up as he held the blade. He breathed deeply as if the blade had its own scent. That grin! God have mercy on anyone who had to face that grin…

Oh… right…

The blade danced in his fingers. Cutter lunged forward at blinding speed. Lightning flashed. The rain started falling harder. I cried out as loud as I could. Cutter had carved off my chest, right over my sternum. The exact spot SmashStone had left his burn mark.

"You won't be needing this!" Cutter shouted over the rain. His teeth flashing that wicked grin. He tossed the piece of skin over his shoulder casually.

Thunder roared in. Blood ran down my chest. My shirt, once pristine, was now in tatters. All the beatings, the scrapes, the cuts. Now the blood trickled down it freely.

Friday let go of my shoulder. All I could do was lean. Which direction would I fall?

"Which do you fear more, brat!" Cutter shouted again. He pulled his fedora even lower over his head so the rain spilled out the front. He stepped closer to me, kicking the waterlogged file out of the way. He put that blade right. Up. To. My. Throat. "Me, or the fall?"

I chose the fall.

I leaned back as far as I could, bound hands raised above my head. Cutter crackled joyously. The world spun around me. My greatest fear. I was in free fall.

Chapter Nine

It takes about four and a half seconds to fall off a skyscraper. Many people have asked what that's like… But really. There's not enough time to think. At least, not like you normally do. It's like your brain registers that it's your last moments on earth and it transcends language.

As I fell, I recognized where I was. Friday had dragged me up the tallest building in the Heap. The Dwight Building.

The wind was buffeting me, pushing me sideways and slowing me.

The fall wasn't as bad as I'd always imagined. My heart. It wasn't beating hard. If anything, I felt calmer and more relaxed than I ever did on the ground. I felt at peace. This was how I would die.

And I was okay with it.

The city, rushing at me. Lightning flashing. It didn't look like I was falling. It looked like I was flying. The ground getting closer wasn't me about to hit it. It was the city that was flying towards me.

The city was falling.

And I wanted to catch it.

I reached out with my hands to try and I felt something *else* reach out too. My shirt ripped away from my back. I felt muscles I'd never felt before.

The wind shifted, the muscles snapped taught and I was off! Shooting past the building, climbing higher and higher. Moving faster than the wind! I really *was* flying!

I had wings! Glorious, beautiful, bronze feathered wings!

They pulled me higher, and higher! High enough to reach the clouds! Lightning flashed, lancing down from on high to the world below, and I saw it for the first time! The City! Briar City. Larger than I could ever have imagined.

Oh, maps could never do this place justice! The Heap, some eighty blocks of mangled, ruined buildings, was nothing but a pimple compared to the majesty of the whole! Cars ran on the roads below, tiny yellow *ants* running along the veins of the city. The place was so *big* and I'd only ever seen so *little* of it. For a moment, I'd forgotten how to breathe.

It was then the wind picked up, the rain washed down even harder, and I was dragged back down in an undercurrent.

Even being tossed around, I was ecstatic. A needle-like spire rose out of the murky haze surrounding me, and I easily powered my way out of the current. I landed on the spire. A giant hole was carved in the side to reduce the wind pressure on it. There was a tiny little nook that I could sense was out of the wind.

I tucked myself into it. My wings folded around me like a blanket. I could sleep here until morning. And then? I didn't know. I couldn't think. The only thing I knew was that Sam Farsight was dead, and I... I was *free*!

Chapter Ten

I woke up the next morning freezing my ass off. Literally. My makeshift cocoon canvassed most of my body, but my butt wasn't one of them. The bitterly cold wind made the whole building as cold as ice. My pants, soaked as they were from sweat, blood, and who knows what else, did nothing to stop my legs from freezing. If I didn't want the world's most bizarre case of frostbite, I had to get up and move around.

I must've spent a good ten minutes just trying to free myself from the restraints. The wings didn't help matters.

Imagine, if you will, having two giant arms sprouting out of your back. These arms each wriggling wildly as I tried to focus on my two normal arms. That's kinda what it was like to untie myself. They kept getting in my way, shifting, and causing me to fall over while I worked.

It's like when you sit down with your palms on a table and you try to lift your third finger without moving your pinky. It takes some getting used to.

Eventually, I pulled my arms free of the duct tape and quickly ripped off the tape around my legs. The gag, if you're curious, came loose during the flight last night. *Good riddance.*

Now that I was freed, I had the chance to truly marvel at my new appendages. Each wing was as long as I was tall. I had so many feathers! Long, bronze feathers; short, tawny feathers. I didn't know what they were individually called, but I could feel each and every one of them if I focused. More than that, with a well-placed thought, I could flex them, too.

I tried shifting the wings in close. The feathers all slid together smoothly. Tucked away as they were, I looked like I had a lumpy backpack over my shoulders. If only I could keep everyone at a distance, I'd be set.

I stretched the wings out wide. It was no different than if I'd just stretched out my arms. The tip of one wing crossed out past the little calm spot I was sitting in and caught the wind. A small gust pulled me out of the calm spot. Once I was exposed, all that wind nearly blew me out of the building! Instinctively, I folded the wings all the way down. Instead of catching the current, the wing acted like a weight, pushing me down against the floor so I could crawl back to the calm spot.

I could see the wind.

I could see it… and *feel* how the wind flowed around me. You know that feeling you get when the hairs on your arms stand on end and you can feel when someone's breathing on you? It's like that times a thousand. Once I fell back into the calm spot, I could even see my breath as it billowed out of my mouth and dissipated into the air currents.

I thought it was the *height* of coolness.

On a whim, I tried wrapping my wings around me like a cacoon. The feathers itched a little against my bare chest, but I immediately started feeling warmer. There was a draft at my back. I'd have to find a new shirt soon.

Speaking of shirts and my chest. The place Cutter had carved off me had scabbed over. I could just barely fit my hand over the spot. Only a tiny point at the bottom stuck out. It itched like crazy now that I was thinking about it. I may have failed Bio101, but I wasn't dumb enough to start scratching it. I remember thinking it was odd that such a serious wound had already begun to heal.

I wasn't in agonizing pain anymore. My arms were stiff, my legs hurt when I tried to wiggle my toes. My lungs caught when I took half a full breath. But I was in much better shape than last night.

The line Bridgess traced across my throat with his knife was completely healed. I couldn't even feel the place where he cut me. All the cuts and scrapes on my arms looked mostly healed, even though they were still tender. A bruise on my side had turned blue. It was sore to touch. I remembered cutting my hand over the knuckles after Friday grabbed me. Now, that same injury was only a white line I could see if I balled my fist up tight.

I was in much better shape than I had any right to be in. After the beatings I took, I should've been hospitalized for a month… But then again… I'm no doctor. All I really knew about my injuries was that they hurt a lot. If my ribs had truly been broken as I thought, would I have still been able to do *any* of the things I did?

I'm not the guy to answer that. Whatever happened yesterday, I felt so much better today that I thought I could risk jumping down off the building.

Bad move.

I walked right over to the edge, pushing against the wind, and looked down. Immediately, I was struck by a wave of vertigo. I stumbled back from the edge. Maybe jumping off the building wasn't the best idea I could've had. I could just take off from the tower. I could deal with my fear once I got in the air. With my wings lifting me, I should be able to just glide down. Gently.

I looked over my shoulder to reassure myself. Instead of being comforted, a sour pit grew in my stomach.

My wings were gone!

"No, no, no!" I shouted to myself. "They can't be gone, they *can't*."

I tried reaching behind me to feel the place the wings connected to my back, but there was nothing to feel. All I managed to do was pull my already sore arms.

The panic quickly passed, however. When I thought about what it felt like to flap my wings, they burst out of my back like confetti, leaving several loose feathers at my feet. This time, they caught the full force of the current around me and pulled me out into the open air.

I was flying again! Once more, it felt as though I'd left all my problems behind. Nothing could stop me now that I was in the sky. Even my vertigo couldn't reach me. What a rush! Now that I was flying, nothing was beyond my power. I was drunk with delight. This was the first of many times I noticed a distinct difference in myself when I was in the air.

I flew up as high as I could. Briar City sprawled out beneath me. Over the city in the East, the sun slowly worked its way up the sky. To the South, the

Heap awaited my return. To the North, the tallest of buildings rose up from the ground, massive skyscrapers so tall the clouds passed through them. And in the West, the ocean stretched out as far as the eye could see.

It dawned on me as I passed ten thousand feet that I could go anywhere. I was free. I could do anything.

There was only one place I wanted to go.

Chapter Eleven

Getting home wasn't so easy. Sure, I found my house easy enough. In the air, traversing the city was as fast as a snap. The hardest part of flying through a back alley was landing without being seen… or heard. Trashcans are my second worst enemy. Especially the tin ones. I swear someone deliberately made those things light and noisy just to screw with me… One bad wing flap and they go banging for miles and miles… Many sneaky missions were ruined because of those damn things.

It was still pretty early in the morning. I didn't have a watch; my best guess was sometime around five. Almost everyone I knew would still be asleep. If I hurried, I could make it upstairs in time for breakfast.

I only had to think about pulling my wings in for them to suck into my body. It was a rather peculiar sensation. In the days to come, I'd practice stretching my wings out and pulling them in again. It was a fun way to pass the time when no one was around.

As I jogged up to the front door of our apartment, I was already thinking of excuses to tell my mom about why I didn't show up last night. I scooped up one of the newspapers thrown lazily into a pile at the foot of our apartment on the way. It would save me from making a trip back down once I got to the top.

I glanced at the headline article. "*Murdered by the Gangs: Boy Discovers Drug Stash and Used as Pawn.*" I couldn't believe my eyes. There was even a picture of me taken straight off of my student I.D. My arms shook as I unfolded the paper to read the rest of the article. A squirming worm of dread in my stomach told me I already knew what it was going to say. What else could it be? Somehow, it never occurred to me that what I did would affect people, besides myself and the gangs. I had to force myself to stop shaking and focus on the first words.

"Sam Farsight, 21, was unlucky enough to discover the SmashStone's drug stash in Wearhouse 15. Stolen only five days prior by the BloodBlades, young Sam Farsight was in the wrong place at the wrong time to witness the brutes hide their contraband. The result? SmashStone and his goons kidnapped the poor boy on his way to college.

"Afterwards, the boy escaped, only to be captured yet again by the BloodBlades and tortured, ending with him being tossed off the roof of the

Dwight building. His body has yet to surface, likely due to last night's heavy storms.

"Yin, of Yin's Noodles, was the first person to notice something was wrong. Said Yin, 'I saw Sammy walking off to school like he always does, but when he walked by me again two hours later, I knew something was bad, wrong. He was drenched in blood and walked like the devil himself was chasing him.'

"No one else in the schools or at the bus stop noticed anything. Was young Sam a victim of circumstance? Judging from how little evidence was left at the scene of the abduction, no. This had to have been planned to absolute perfection. Said a police spokesperson, 'It's always tragic to lose such a promising individual. But there was simply no way of knowing [Sam Farsight] was in trouble. Thousands of young men lose their way in the Heap every day.'

"But is this the truth? Confidential information has it on good authority that the police knew of Sam Farsight's predicament. Yin originally reported the incident at one o'clock—well before the boy met his tragic end.

"Both gangs met in a climactic showdown deep within the bowels of Wearhouse 15 at nine that evening. A showdown that resulted in three gang members being hospitalized, five locked up (thanks to the interference of a vigilante on the scene), and seven deaths — including the deaths of young Mr.

Farsight and of the notorious Seth Bridgess. Police claim this incident spontaneously occurred when the SmashStones invaded the BloodBlades secret storehouse. But, approximately one hour before the first shots were fired, an anonymous source called the police with detailed information leading to the cops' full arrest of everyone involved.

"Was this call made by Sam Farsight? Was it a cry for help? Or could it have been the work of the rumored rogue, DinoHyde, said to stalk Barron Corp territory like Wearhouse 15?

"This case has far more questions than answers. Chief among them: Why didn't Sam Farsight trust the cops with this information in the first place? And what exactly was the delay in investigating Sam Farsight's case?

"All we can say for sure is that this was a preventable crime, and Sam Farsight paid the price for our negligence."

I read and re-read the article five times before it sunk in. *I was officially dead.* There was even a hotline set up for people to pay respects and help fund the funeral… or call in my body, if found…

Who could've told the reporters all this? All it said in the article was "confidential sources." Perhaps DinoHyde had left them the information? Or Martin?? It was *almost* right. Like some parts of the story were deliberately changed to make me look like the victim, instead of the instigator. Why would any of them protect me like that? As far as they knew, I was dead.

… Still… My mother could go on believing that I'd died trapped in a bad situation instead of…

Whoever changed the article tried to do me a favor. I supposed I owed them…

But. There was no returning to my life. If I did, it would make even bigger headlines. Everyone would want to know how I survived getting chucked off a building. They'd ask questions I wouldn't feel comfortable answering. The world would eventually find out about my wings. And then what? Would anyone let me live a normal life?

More likely they'd lock me in a lab somewhere and dissect me. They'd label me a security risk and throw me in an underground prison for the rest of my days. The government can be strangely predictable like that.

Reading my obituary made things… final. After that, I could never be a normal person again. My life as Sam Farsight was truly over. And if I wanted to keep my new life, I'd have to do it on my own.

I needed time to think. Time to figure out what was safe… and what would get me killed…

I dropped the paper where I'd read it and took off back to the alley. I jumped back into the air without even meeting one person — without telling anyone I was still alive. The only person who needed to know was my mom. And I, still to this day, believe she was better off thinking I died.

Chapter Twelve

The next few months were harsh. I had nothing — no money, no clothes, just the one pair of pants on my legs and the two shoes on my feet. I didn't have any supplies. I didn't have any gear. The only thing I could hope for was to sit in a public place with the last tattered rags of my shirt over my face and beg people for money to eat.

Some people were kind. Others… not so much. I wasn't shy about begging, though, which helped me a lot. People also seemed to think my face was deformed, thanks to the rags. I never corrected them. I just accepted their money, used it to get proper clothes, and, when I had enough, a backpack and a sleeping bag.

I had the power to go anywhere in the world. But I had nowhere to go. I had the strength to do anything I wanted to do, but all I wanted to do was survive.

It doesn't take a person much to survive if they can fly. I could go anywhere in the city in a matter of minutes. All I needed was a backpack, a mask, a few changes of clothes… and a place to sleep. Ironically, I slept far better outdoors than I ever had inside. Just a tarp over my sleeping bag, and I was set for rain or shine. If I couldn't find a place to sleep on the ground, there was always an empty rooftop ready to accommodate me. Everything had workarounds I could exploit.

I spent an entire month living like this. Only really flying at dusk, when everyone went to sleep, or morning before the sun rose completely. The rest of the time was mine to do with as I pleased… Mostly, to think.

I was officially homeless. The others in the homeless community barely seemed to notice me… but they accepted me, mask and all.

I watched my family from a distance. A big distance. Every time I found one excuse to make contact… I found twelve more to stay away.

I should've found a way. I could've… if I'd set my mind to it. Twenty years later and it's still my only real regret… Maybe nothing would've changed at all. I don't know.

Once, I tried to find DinoHyde or the Runner to see if they'd help me, but… they were gone. I couldn't find any trace of them. Getting back into Wearhouse 15 proved impossible. The police kept the place locked up tighter than a CEO's coin purse. But no one knew about the building DinoHyde "interrogated" me on; unfortunately, there was nothing to find there. A couple of skid marks from my chair. My extraordinary, magical powers of deduction deduced that someone had tied me up there.

My resolve didn't get truly tested again until the day of my funeral. It happened one month after my "death." I guess they were still hoping they could find a body to bury… Sorry to disappoint.

Of course, I watched my own funeral, how could I not? Rooftops were plentiful, and the skies were clear as crystal. My mother, brother, and cousins were all in attendance. Even a few people I knew from school.

My mother cried… a lot… That's fair, I cried a lot too. I was too far away to hear what they said. But I could see everyone walk forward and leave flowers. I could imagine what everyone was saying. And their every word hollowed out my insides.

I wanted so much to tell them I was still alive… But… The gangs were leaving them alone. They could live in peace because Cutter and SmashStone both thought I was personally touring Heaven… All it would take is *one* person to find out the truth and spill it by accident.

I had to stay as far away as I could. That was the only way to protect them.

The next few months hurt even worse.

I took up alcohol as a hobby. You'd be amazed how easy it is for a resourceful young beggar to find a sip without an ID. Especially one who can fly and create gusts of air with his wings. I must've lost a whole extra month singing karaoke with a bottle… Even on nights when they had the machine turned off…

I guess you could say I was mourning Sam Farsight… I-I like to *t-think* I was mourning Sam Farsight… Died before his time… Too young… *much* too young…

Alcohol's potent stuff. Some nights, I even forgot I had wings.

But I remembered in the morning. I *always* remembered in the morning.

I'd walk the streets and think, *What was I doing here?* Why, out of all people, why was *I* blessed with an honest-to-God superpower? What good is one college drop-out going to do in the world? Even if he did have wings.

It was those early mornings that nearly killed me. Closer than any bullet. Deeper than any knife. Because something would happen in those early mornings. Something that drove me back to the nearest bottle. I dreaded it every morning… or… perhaps I wanted it instead? It was an instinct. Calling out for me. Calling me to do something that terrified me.

Every morning. The air would get quiet. So quiet you could hear a leaf falling in a yard. So quiet you could hear a person turning a page in a book. The quiet was like a church. Like a library. It was reverent. A spiritual time.

And the sounds of sirens would disturb it.

What was I supposed to do? What the *hell* was I supposed to do?!? Sit back and watch? *I refuse*!! One crime happens every minute in the city. The police can't stop it—No one can stop it. Crime will always find a way…

But you can save someone's life. Right? People don't have to die. The Sam Farsight's of the world don't have to perish getting chucked off buildings. The Jerry Brighart's of the world don't have to wind up on the wrong ends of a shooting, do they?? N-not if there's someone to catch them. Are you supposed to just let the bad things happen? I couldn't—No—*I can't believe that*. I can't! No matter what he says! Everyone deserves a chance at life! Everyone deserves to live a full and free life. No… no more kids in caskets…

But… how exactly was *I* supposed to save lives?? All of my talents could only make things worse. The world needed a *real* hero. Not some boozer with chicken wings. The cops knew what they were doing, didn't they? Of course they did—they're cops! Who would want some washed-up failure to come to save them with his hangover that could crack concrete?

Well… people in trouble—real trouble… they might want help… And they might not be too picky about where that help came from. A-and… cops aren't always the most reliable when it comes to saving people who need it. But a person with wings…

I could get to the people who needed me… and be back losing my mind in a large cuppa in the same time it took a commercial to play during a football game.

It would almost be *irresponsible* of me to *not go*, wouldn't it? I mean, j-just to check out what was happening. Right? Lord in Heaven, please let it be something simple. M-maybe no one would need me at all. Maybe drinking a cuppa—or two—was just what the doctor ordered.

Every day since I found my wings, I walked down the street in the mornings. It was always a different street… but it was the same street. The same conversations… the same argument. Over. And over… and *over*. And then, to change things up, I'd have it over again. And once more just to torture myself.

The last time I got involved with things I didn't understand, I killed someone: *me!*

Going back was no easy task.

But, on the other hand… if a horse bucks you off…

What harm would there be in just walking over to wherever the sirens are? What harm is there in looking? I mean, if it's nothing serious I could always walk away and let the cops handle it, right?? Just looking—I don't have to step in.

I have never, in all my life, ridden a horse before, but I knew sooner or later I'd wear the cowl. Was I ready for it? Was the city ready for me to wear it?

Damn it! How could anyone just let people die! How could you! How…

I would've drunk a whole vat full of poison if it would just stop the questions. I would've…

They say real men don't cry… I guess that makes me less than a man—because I did. Every time I turned away. Every time I found a drink to drown myself in. Every damn time I heard those sirens… I cried. And then I'd drink some more and the cycle would continue one more day. And then one more…

One day—one fucking *terrible* day—I found myself wishing I'd just died when I tumbled off that building. Cutter couldn't have made me suffer worse. Not with a thousand knives.

Maybe that's why… that day… I didn't run away from the sirens. Maybe… I didn't care that it might kill me for real anymore. Maybe I was just sick to death of trying to break my moral compass with a bottle. I think… somehow… I reached a point where my spirit couldn't take running away again. Not one more time.

So I followed the sirens instead.

Chapter Thirteen

A whole road was blocked off. The police had gathered with heavy vests and hoards of vans labeled S.W.A.T. I couldn't see past the boys in blue. One officer, a woman who I later found out was named Nancy Green, was waving people back even as more cops arrived on the scene.

Boy, I sure know how to pick disasters, don't I?

I had long ago traded the rags on my face for a black ski mask. People didn't look at me quite so sadly… or as often when I wore the mask. If I kept my head down, I could all but disappear in a crowd. Besides, ski masks were *in* amongst the homeless fashion shows of the season.

I wormed my way through the crowd and ducked behind an ally. Using my wings, I half flew, half jumped up the nearest building. It was only three stories tall, but I needed to see what was going on. The small building would do just fine for that.

Few things inspire terror like a city block full of cops. They blocked all four of the roads surrounding the square. As far as I could see, seven rooftops carried police snipers, all aimed at the grand building in the center.

First National. I'd stumbled across a bank robbery.

Real sudden like, I was on a different rooftop, with a different robbery in mind. The night Cutter carved off my chest. His laugh, and the flash of thunder. Friday dragging me up and letting me fall. DinoHyde growling "This isn't a game, brat!"

I fell flat on my *derie-air* and tossed my cookies. Luckily, my wings were pulled in. I do not want to think about how frustrating it would be to clean vomit off of them...

"What am I thinking?!?" I exclaimed to myself. "Just fly over there in plain view of a million trigger happy cops and ask the bank robbers inside to ignore me while I fly away with the hostages? Yeah, what could *possibly* go wrong with that plan—Besides everything!"

If the cops hadn't just busted in there already, it meant the bank robbers had hostages and knew every trick the cops had tried so far... But it wouldn't take long before they reached the point of no return. Before the cops rushed in, guns blazing. Hostages be damned...

There was a surge of reporters down in the streets below. Their poor cameramen. I doubt they'd ever get a good shot from the street. Nothing but bad angles. It would be the reporters in the air that got their time in the limelight…

"Where are the choppers?" I asked myself. There wasn't a helicopter in sight. Not a one. Not even for the local news—clear skies as far as the eye could see… or hear…

All of a sudden, I had a terrible, stupid plan.

Behind me, the stairwell door opened. A fresh-faced young cop stepped into the sunlight, looking every inch the model officer. From his short blonde hair, right on down to the freckles on his face. As if they came with his diploma from the police academy.

"What the—This building's been cleared for police use only. You're under arrest for obstruction, pal." He started for his sidearm, forgetting for a moment that he wasn't using the normal gear and that his only weapon was still in its case.

"Sorry," I said, stepping towards the roof. "I'll just—I'll be going now." I jumped off the edge.

The young cop shouted, "Wait!" and rushed after me. But by the time he got to the guardrail, I was already flying as fast as I could to the bank. Praying every second that I wasn't about to get shot in the... *everywhere* — by trigger-happy cops.

I landed on the roof without a hitch. *Phase one, complete*, I thought. Now I just had to make up phases two through four. And hope there wasn't a phase five I needed to make up too.

In theory, the thugs inside weren't watching the skies. They were *listening*. Helicopters make a lot of noise. If one even took off within seven blocks, everyone would know it before the thing even lifted off the ground. If these guys were smart and planned for this...

I just needed to find a way in.

To my great surprise, one such way was already available; a skylight had been opened.

It didn't take much effort to shimmy my way down into the building. I was in some kind of accounting room. There was a desk with a computer and a bunch of filing cabinets, but not much else.

The door was left wide open. I was following somebody.

"I said 'quiet!'" a rough voice called out.

One of the bank robbers. His call didn't help much; I could still hear the hostages whimpering from all the way in my backroom.

I walked to the atrium… Slowly. It would be just my luck that one of the robbers opened that hatch during some kind of patrol and he would make his way back any second…

I didn't bother putting my wings away. They might not be so useful indoors, but they made me look bigger. It might take someone by surprise… Maybe.

The hallway opened onto the second floor of the atrium. I hit a snag. Zero cover. The glass walkway wrapped around the walls and sloped down to the ground floor. There were big glass wraparound windows near the bottom. Not only could the robbers use it to check on the police outside, but it let in a lot of natural light. I'd be spotted instantly if I moved past the doorway. And unless the glass was bulletproof—which I doubted—I was whiffed.

I looked across the opening desperately. There had to be something—anything—I could use as cover. But there was nothing. My only hope was to hide in the shadows of the doorway and pray one of them was dumb enough to walk up there on his own.

And then I saw it. I looked up in frustration and saw the molded rafters. It would only just barely be big enough to hide behind... but better than nothing.

I never tried that jumping trick indoors before. There was no way of telling what side effects could happen. For a brief second, I worried that jumping might give the whole game away. What if the cheap facade groaned when I landed on it? I'd be full of holes faster than I could think *oops*.

But there wasn't any other option if I wanted to be of any use to anyone.

I braced myself. And jumped.

My foot stepped on to the rafter as if I'd just walked up to it. Not a creek to be heard… Unfortunately, the gust created by my wings blew through the atrium like a thunderstorm.

"What the hell was that?" One of the thugs shouted, swinging his gun wildly, looking for something to shoot.

From my new perch, I could see everything. Eight hostages, four robbers. The robbers were almost as well equipped as the police force outside their doors. All four of them carried military-grade body armor and rifles. Their faces were covered by ski masks not too much different from my own. One hostage was trapped with a robber behind the register…

And one man lay on the floor… in a pool of blood… he wasn't breathing…

You could see the tension in the room had gone up a notch. The hostages didn't make a sound. A woman in blue pushed herself up against the wall. She had both her hands clamped over her mouth as if her life depended on it.

"Maybe it was an open window?" One of the robbers covering the hostages spoke up. He was focused completely on the hostages, watching their every move. Of the four, he was the smallest of the bunch. I mean it, the guy was *super* tiny. He was almost as small as…

As… … me…

"Can't be," said the guy covering the door. He was jacked. His arms alone were nearly twice the size of an average man of his height. "I checked all the backrooms. I locked this place up tighter than a cork in a bottle of wine."

"Well, maybe you missed something!" the small guy insisted.

"Both of you, shut up!" The guy behind the register commanded. "It sounds like we've got company."

"God, I hope it's the Runner," the last thug spoke up. He was piling money in black duffel bags and passing two to each crook. "I still owe him for shoving me off that bridge."

"I don't care who it is, if anyone walks through that door, you turn 'im into swiss cheese."

The fourth robber finished putting all the money in their bags. He and the man at the door trained their guns at the doorway on the second floor.

I froze stiff. My wings were half tucked behind me. I didn't dare move them an inch. Not even a feather. They grew heavier every second I stood there behind the facade. I thought for sure the gunmen could see me. The big one by the door looked right at me. He stared me square in the eye! I didn't so much as breathe until he looked away.

I could see the eddies from my jump still cycling around the room. The air tends to just keep moving in a round room. It keeps cycling for longer. The currents… linger. It makes it easier to create bigger gusts.

I was still working out how to use this as a distraction when I was spared having to do anything at all.

While the robbers focused on the doorway underneath me, a man appeared out of nowhere at the foot of the walkway. I don't know how he did it, but somehow he hid even from my sharp eyes.

No one had any time to react. He pulled out his bow and shot an arrow in the center of the room. He was dressed in a flamboyant red outfit. Cargo jeans with combat boots. He had enough spare quivers sewn into his shirt that it was virtually impossible to count the arrows.

"It's Hotshot Lagoon!" one robber shouted in warning—but he was too late! Fast as thought, Hotshot launched a series of arrows that knocked the guns away from three of the four thugs. The man behind the register ducked to the gate and opened fire wildly.

In the center, the first arrow fired released a thick, white cloud that quickly filled the room in a murky haze. Tear gas. I was safe. From my perch, I had plenty of time to cover my mouth and squint my eyes. The robber behind the register wasn't so lucky and got himself a face-full of the chemical.

Hotshot tossed two of the thugs away from the door. The smallest thug pulled out his handgun, but Hotshot knocked him down to the ground and disarmed him.

"Run—Quickly!" He told the hostages while he drew another arrow. The other hostages obeyed him readily enough. Not that he noticed. Hotshot was already moving on with his arrow to take out the man behind the register.

Only two hostages remained behind. One, the woman behind the register. She lay on the floor, her ankle twisted. The other hostage was the woman in blue against the wall. It looked like she also got a face-full of tear gas. She fell to the floor, choking. She wasn't going anywhere quickly.

The big robber pulled himself up and started fishing around for his guns. Hotshot put an arrow in his shin. For some odd reason, the big guy wasn't so interested in fighting anymore. Go figure.

I made my move.

The register was essentially a line of tellers desks behind thick, bullet-proof glass. The only way in or out was through the gate… The gate that the bad guy with the gun was currently guarding…

Unless you could fly.

Dropping in from above, I landed on top of the teller.

"Hold on! I'll get you out of here!"

Instead of answering, the teller wrapped her arms around my neck tight enough to nearly choke me. Good enough.

I jumped with all my strength, flapping my wings to give me that extra lift. Both Hotshot and the thug at the gate were pushed back. It also had the unfortunate effect of whipping up the extra tear gas around the room again.

I landed next to the last hostage. Shifting the teller into one arm, I threw the other woman over my shoulder.

The short robber came to his senses enough to grab his gun and aim it at me. It looked stupid with an arrow sticking out of it. But it still shot bullets at me.

I leaped up high to the windows with the women still in my arms. At the last second, I wrapped my wings around the three of us. We broke through the glass like a cannonball.

I was off like a shot! Over the police, past the buildings, and down the alleyway. The cop I'd run into on the rooftop looked up from his scope like he couldn't believe his eyes. I waved as we passed him. *Welcome to Briar City.*

The back alley probably wasn't the best place to land with a couple of women after a bank robbery. I knocked over another trashcan with our landing. Classy, right?

"Are you okay?" I asked them both. The lady who inhaled the tear gas looked much better now that we were out in the open. A blast of fresh air while being carried like a sack of potatoes will do that to you.

"I-I think so," she answered. The other lady—the teller—she only nodded, her eyes wide open. Together, they managed to stand up, the teller leaning on the other. Both of them were quivering… And… I don't think it was out of admiration… To be fair, if some strange man picked *me* up out of a robbery with his wings… Yeah, I'd be pretty fricken terrified too.

"Good—" I started. But before I could finish an arrow shot right through my shoulder.

"Run!" I told them, flaring my wings up to give them more cover. They hobbled out of the ally back to the line of police, while I faced my attacker. But when I turned, Hotshot was already putting his bow away.

"*You're* a *hero*?" he asked. It was impossible to miss the incredulous note of condescension in his voice. He sounded less like someone who realized he'd made a mistake and more like a rich brat who discovered that some peasants had to drive *themselves* to school.

"Duh," I returned with equal disdain.

"Oh I'm *sorry*," he japed. "You look like a common street thug—You really ought to wear brighter colors. This outfit is the work of an amateur—and I must say—a piss-poor one at that. A hero needs to stand out against the throes of villainy! It should be distinct and immediately apparent who you are even from a distance!"

I flexed my wings pointedly. "Yeah, I'll keep that in mind the next time I'm with my personal tailor."

Hotshot nodded. "Very good—you're mocking me, aren't you?"

"You did just *shoot me in the arm*," I reminded him nastily. Now that the adrenalin was wearing off, I could feel the dull throb from the arrow. It wasn't helping my mood.

"Pish, posh!" Hotshot scoffed. "I've shot *myself* worse than that. Just break off the tip, remove the shaft, and the wound should heal up in a couple of days."

"Rrrright. Look, I have a busy day of getting drunk off my socks to get back to. Thanks for the souvenir, but I really must be going now. Sir." I threw as much sarcasm into the 'sir' as I could to be as much of an insolent bastard as it's possible to be.

It got Hotshot's attention. The archer looked disgruntled for a minute and then snapped his fingers. "I've got it. Here. Come here."

"You're not going to shoot me again, are you?" I asked warily. Shoot me once…

Hotshot waved my barb aside casually. It was… *probably* safe to approach him. So I did. He pulled out a small, plain white business card and wrote an address on it.

"Here," he said, giving it to me. "This place used to be the lair for a vigilante hero. The Fab Master. He was a costume maker who died in the Great Corporate War. Some of us older hero's make sure the place stays well-stocked. He was an adamant anti-capitalist, so to keep his spirit alive we sometimes wave newbies down there for their hero suits."

I was floored. The Fab Master was a legend! He fought for the gay and trans communities in a time where being gay was enough to warrant execution by the gangs. I had no idea that he was a costume maker… but it explained a lot about the hero suits from that era. And I was just handed the address to his old lair…

"I—Thank you!" I said sincerely.

Hotshot nodded sagely. "Yes. There are a few rules we expect, of course. Don't go there if the cops are searching for you. Same with bad guys.

And no staying overnight. No one knows the place is still operating; it needs to stay that way."

I nodded to show I was listening. Those seemed to be pretty fair rules to me.

"Also, we don't mind you using any of the suits or materials but don't steal or break any of the equipment. We will hunt you down and take it out of your hide. Do you think that arrow hurts now? Wait until I put it somewhere important.

"Aside from that, the only other rule is no fighting. If your worst villain walks into the place; you leave it at the door."

"No breaking the equipment."

"Precisely. That place holds a lot of memories for all of us. The suits there are parts of our legacy. Special orders. Old styles. A few custom items—used for a specific rogue and never needed again. That sort of thing."

"I understand. I'll treat it like a church."

Hotshot grimaced, "Fab Master would've died at the irony of that."

He turned to walk away and thought better of it. "One more thing! If you use a retired hero's costume…"

"I'll try to bring honor to their memory," I promised.

Hotshot looked satisfied. "Good luck, newbie."

Before I could wish him the same, a voice called out over a megaphone. "Don't move *heroes*. You're under arrest." From behind me, several cops filed into the ally. Cutting off any chance I had of walking out of there.

"That's my cue to leave!" Hotshot announced.

What happened next was entirely my fault. I started to ask what he meant by that… at the same time, Hotshot dropped a smoke bomb. Because, *of course*, he would drop a smoke bomb. The hero's *always* dropped a smoke bomb when they were surrounded. My dumb ass got a nice mouthful of the stuff instead of air.

I coughed and sputtered on the ground just like the rest of the cops. By the time I made it to my feet, tears in my eyes, one man, a little better dressed than the others, put his gun to my face.

"Randal Dreg, FBI," he announced. The other officers deferred to his authority. "Hotshot got away, but we caught ourselves a little pigeon."

"I'm not a pigeon!"

"You don't get any say in the matter. Criminals don't get to choose their nicknames; *I do*. You should feel honored, bird boy. I've caught some of the greats. Much bigger and better heroes than you'll ever be. Wild Thunder. SlingShot. The Dodger. All of them carried themselves with dignity that you can't ever hope to match."

"You're the Catcher?"

"So you've heard of me?" Randal Dreg—the Catcher, looked pleased with himself. I guess the guy had to get in his kicks somehow. He was always the boogeyman in all the hero stories. When the heroes messed up or did villainy, he was the guy who stepped in at the end of the story to lock them up. Nobody lived happily-ever-after in those stories.

"Is it true you once stole Christmas from a village living in a snowflake?"

"Yes," he answered without skipping a beat. "Now then, cage the bird would you?" He asked one of the SWAT agents next to him.

"Are the hostages safe?" I asked as the guy drew closer to me. He shrugged. The Catcher brushed aside my concerns.

"There was one casualty in the bank, the teller wouldn't do as the gunmen asked. But the two ladies you pulled out are fine—no thanks to you. You nearly scared those two girls half to death. Dragging them through a window like that."

"Not my fault. The bad guys had *guns*, you know." I twitched my wings indignantly.

It wasn't a conscious move. Just a reflex. Do you know how some people start grinding their teeth when they're frustrated? I flex my wings. There's nothing violent about it... Anyone with any sense could see I was harmless...

The cops... didn't...

Everyone except special agent Dreg fired their rifles right in my face! Point blank. The Catcher tried hard to make himself heard over the gunfire. "Hold your fire! For God's sake, hold your fire!" But none of them did.

You may have noticed I'm writing this twenty years later. No, I'm not so full of holes you could use me for a colander… but I should be.

When the cops opened fire, I curled up and tucked my head away from the violence. Another reflex thing. I also folded my wings around the front of my body. No one was more surprised than I to find out my wings were bulletproof. No one else was quite as elated as I was either.

The Catcher, who, before the others opened fire, was standing right in front of me, was now—understandably—a few steps away. Shell casings and flattened bullets peppered the ground between us.

For a solid minute, no one said anything. We were all in shock. Me, the Catcher, and about twenty or so SWAT members… just staring in disbelief. I was the one who cautiously broke the silence.

"I-uh… left the oven on… gotta-go-bye." I took off. Jumped right over their heads and flew away as fast as I could. One guy dropped his gun uselessly, followed a second later by his jaw. A single feather landed right over the Catcher's head.

Chapter Fourteen

Fab Master's lair was quite nice.

As requested, I waited a day before seeking it out. I disposed of the clothes I was wearing during the robbery. As plain as I looked, there was no chance of the cops finding me, but it never hurt to be cautious. I traded the jeans with a hobo down near the pier. The shoes I swapped for a pair of boots. And the shirt found a nice home with Kenny Durben, though he *did* wonder why two massive holes were cut into the back. I told him I stole it from someone who mugged someone else for it. Kenny, bless his soul, always was a touch… slow. But he always dealt fairly with me.

It took just about the whole day to change all my clothes.

The address on the card led to an old abandoned store on the East End.

Lots of shops down on the East End. Most of them sprang up after the Corporate War. Young hopefuls, the lot of them; all eager to prove that capitalism wasn't so bad, that anyone could make it with some good Old-American gumption. Some people did do well for themselves… usually white people. (But I'm sure that's just a coincidence.) There's a lot of family businesses that are still going strong now in their second or even third generation.

But there's also a lot of empty stores.

The Green Emperor looked to be just another empty store. But unlike the other boarded-up stores, this one still opened when you pulled the handle. The fake boards across her front opened up without even a squeak at the hinges.

Inside the store was a deep, luscious red velvet carpet. I must've sunk three inches in it. It was that soft. A polished oak countertop stretched out in front of me. Three stools spaced evenly created a comfortable space for clients. To my left were the dirtiest windows you'll ever see! They let light in, but you couldn't see out of them to save your life. Under the circumstances, I counted them as a blessing. To my right, there was a small dining room and stairs to an upper level.

There was a small bell on the countertop. Like a dumbass, I rang it. I'll let you guess how long I stood there waiting before I remembered that the place was abandoned…

The costumes had to be in the back room. Sure enough, there was another hidden door on the other side of the countertop. The inside of this room was pitch black.

I felt along the wall and found a lever much like the one Terry Mac pulled back in the Rock bar… Bad memories—I couldn't shake the feeling SmashStone was about to jump down from the ceiling… I pulled the lever up, and the lights turned on.

This side was much less extravagant than the business side. Concrete floors, crude wooden stools, but the seven racks of hero suits more than made up for the lack of creature comforts. Each rack was divided between masculine & feminine designs and carried faded labels that proved impossible to read no matter how much I squinted at them.

I recognized a lot of suits: Here was one used by Action, one of the Runner's predecessors. Another suit used to belong to WildThing, who ran around as a cave-man neanderthal before he retired. (I even found his club in a box underneath the suit.)

One shock was recognizing a suit belonging to the Sphinx! Somehow her miniskirt and "busty" top made it into the masculine section of costumes. I hoped that was either a mistake or a joke. Fab Master seemed to have the suits organized by gender presentation, so it didn't make sense it would be in the wrong aisle. Most likely, some newbie hero like myself pulled it out of its place and forgot where it went.

There was an entire section of hero suits modified for formal occasions: dresses and four-piece tuxedos that made you look elegant while still carrying all your butt-kicking needs. With a gasp, I recognized Miss Diva's wedding gown, complete with two sets of shoes (for dancing or walking the aisle) and a harness under the dress to hold throwing knives.

On the walls, there were pictures of all the big heroes in their suits. Some of them were signed and dated, and Fab Master was in all of them. In his day suit, he didn't look all that extraordinary. Truth be told, he looked a bit on the dweeb-y side… Tweed shirts and ugly sweaters. Slacks, but not the hip "I'm just being flamboyant" kind, more the ugly, tan, "I can do your taxes too" kind. Thick, round glasses that wouldn't look out-of-place on a nerd in the 1900's. The man even had a pocket protector for Pete's sake!

There were hundreds of suits on the racks… But not one of them was for me. That damned instinct that drove me to chase the sirens now kept telling me, *not this one*. These were all old suits for old heroes. They'd seen their heyday. They had their time of glory. Me? I was something different. Something new. I'd have to find my own path.

Besides, none of the other suits had holes in their back for my wings.

Moving away from the racks, I dusted off the nearest table. It was marked off in little boxes all across the surface. All one inch long. A box on top of it had protractors, compasses, rulers, tapes—just about everything a person would need to measure. Down a few tables was a sewing machine, stocked with thread of all sizes and more needles than one voodoo doll could ever hold.

In short, everything I'd need to make my own superhero suit. There was only one problem: I had no idea how to sew.

I tried a cabinet in the corner. Inside were stacks upon stacks of every kind of sewing manual imaginable.

It's a good thing I like to read…

I ended up breaking that "no staying overnight" rule religiously. It took me *six weeks* just to read through the manuals. In truth, about half of that time was drawing, scrapping, and redrawing the basic designs for my hero suit. By the end of those six weeks, I knew what each of those tables was and how each tool was used. If I needed an example to look at, the hero suits themselves displayed nearly every type of stitching technique imaginable.

About three days in, I discovered a three-ring binder with every blueprint Fab Master had ever drawn, painstakingly laminated and labeled. That in itself was a gold mine of nostalgia and education. Near the back of the binder, I found much cruder blueprints — newer heroes adding their designs to the collection. Before I left, I added my own suit's blueprints to the binder for posterity.

In an eye-opening moment, I got to take a peek at HotShot Lagoon's super suit, drawn in his handwriting. That thing had more hidden pockets than a magician's cloak. And there were even sketches of a camouflaged blanket. No doubt, he perfected the idea over the years and that was how he managed to sneak up on the bank robbers. N-not that that had been bothering me, or anything! I-I knew there had to be some kind of trick to it. People don't just turn invisible… No matter how it might've looked at the time…

HotShot wanted this place to stay off the radar, I obliged. I slept in the backroom. Begged and ate my lunches outside. I did my business in the local library. I even made sure all the lights were off by sunset, which, to be fair, I probably didn't have to do, but I didn't want to take the chance someone would see the lights on in the building.

Designing my suit was no easy task; I was having a hard time deciding on a motif.

Yeah, I know. *You have wings*! But I didn't want my wings to be the *only* thing that defines me! I toyed around with the idea of using a firefighter theme. There was one kickass water gun for one of the classic heroes. It stored up, like, a hundred gallons of water and released it in a high-powered blast. That gun alone was cool enough to warrant designing a suit around it. I wanted to save people, and firefighters saved lots of people. But I'd never served in the military. And the Old-America Police get pretty aggressive when people impersonate one of their officers.

Eventually, the part of me that didn't want to be shot execution-style live on the evening news caved to the inevitable and started designing around my wings. They w-*are* my greatest asset, you know. I wanted something simple, but cool. Something lightweight and flexible. Something I could build off of later. I didn't have the patience to try to work in some bulletproof feathers immediately, so just a basic hero suit would hold me over until I had the extra time to work on it.

Eventually, after trying every color and every cloth swatch against myself in the full-body mirror, I settled on a dark brown leather that looked good with my complexion and my wings.

I was quite proud of the finished product. The leather stain looked good. It made for a great base to add more color. And, as a bonus, there was a matching set of leather gloves. As for color, I settled on a bright yellow over my front and back that faded into the brown of the leather at my sides. I then outlined each of the stitches with black cloth. It disguised how clumsy my stitching was. The pants were patterned the same way.

There were three metal sheets that I was able to work into the chest piece. According to the books, they wouldn't make me bulletproof, but they would offer some protection against knife wounds and basic punches. Two pieces went into the front of the chest, and one to the back.

By necessity, there's a large hole in the back of my suit where my wings shoot out from. There was only a tiny sliver of my skin exposed between the two wings. That was a spot I couldn't cover easily, no matter how I twisted or folded my wings. That section got the third metal plate.

I stood in front of the mirror and stretched my wings out dramatically. HotShot wanted me to look distinct. I stretched every which way I could think of. A stained leather belt made sure my pants would stay on me as I flew around at high speeds. I pulled my wings around the front of my arms like a cloak. The feathers glinted in the light. Except for the ski mask on my head, I looked like a warrior. A fighter. But if I folded my wings over my shoulder, I looked like a prince.

I managed to stitch together four hidden pockets — two in the chest, on the sides, and one in each leg of the pants. I thought I could stuff a few feathers in them for emergencies, but the first time I tried to pluck one out of the pockets, I turned my hands into so much hamburger—the edges of those things were *sharp*!

A little experimentation and I found I could use one of my feathers just as effectively as any cutter or knife in Fab Master's lair. And the quill ends made for good hole punches, or drills if I gave it a bit of a twist. After that, I reinforced the left leg pocket with extra stitches and added a small loop to keep one feather on me at all times.

The only other thing was my cowl… yikes! That thing never turned out how I wanted it. I was trying to go for some kind of full-faced hawk head, but it was completely impractical; I'd have to keep my eyes clear if I wanted to be able to see. That completely threw off all my designs. And everything I made was about as aerodynamic as a glob of mashed potatoes.

Eventually, I was forced to give it up and just stick with my ski mask. After spending another two months just working on my hero suit… I was getting stir crazy! It was time to get back out there and show the world who's boss!

You know, in two months I hadn't sipped a single drop of alcohol? I managed to give it up. Not permanently, but… now that I was working towards a purpose…

I didn't *need* it like I did before.

I was a superhero in spirit! All my wounds had finally healed, from the triangle scar over my chest to the arrow wound HotShot left me. I had wings to fly, a suit to don, an urge to help, and a can-do attitude!

Now all I needed was someone to pull out of a burning building and my life as a superhero could truly begin.

…

Why did I even *think* that?

Chapter Fifteen

I started my first patrol with the sunrise.

After spending so much time slinking around in the shadows, I was strangely self-conscious of flying in the daytime. Biting the bullet, I changed in an abandoned building, stepped out in the street, and, heedless of who saw me, aimed for the sky, flying straight down the middle of Main Street.

People pointed up at me. They raised their phones to take pictures of me. I zipped by as fast as I could, my cheeks burning every second I thought about the dumb ski mask on my face. Or the hobo boots on my feet.

I tried to focus on finding a crime to stop. This might sound stupid… but after two months of preparing to face the world as a superhero, I still didn't know where all the crime happened. Just my luck… I spent two months straight being bombarded with sirens, but now that I was ready to do something about it—nothing!

I swooped over a low building and surprised the daylights out of a storekeeper messing with his satellite. I didn't stop to chat. He started calling me a devil in Spanish, and I got the impression he wasn't so fond of birds…

Nor was the window-washer I nearly knocked into the street. He only fell for like… *two seconds*. I picked him back up and set him on his little scaffold thing. Right as rain. Did I get a thank you? No… Just a bunch of screaming and swearing.

I started flying into the Brigham District. Upper-class territory. All resorts and casinos. The only crime happening in this district went on inside the buildings… Still, maybe some thugs were hiding in the alleyways? I mean, I knocked over a bunch of paparazzi stalking the high-rise of their favorite actress, but they *could* have been muggers, right? Right??

I found a couple of nude sunbathers who, predictably, started screaming and covering up when I flew headfirst into a tree on the other side of their resort. I guess I had my mind on *other things*…

So much can happen in a city! All this took place in the span of an hour. But still no crime to stop.

At long last, I heard a siren. The cop car was barreling down forty-second street; the engine roared as it cut through traffic. I followed from above. We were heading to the industrial sector at the north end of the city: Exactly one lot devoted to being a park with natural ground... and *lots* of space converted into big factories, power plants, and other manufacturing offices. What few corporations survived the Great Corporate War all had headquarters and business buildings up here. Maybe I was about to be involved with some kind of espionage?

Nope. It was the thirty-fourth annual BCPD's Picnic... Not a single cop nor their family members appreciated me swooping through the middle of their holiday and blowing their BBQ off the grills and into the dirt. Especially the cop in the car... I—uh... *may* have tried to tell him off for using his sirens irresponsibly. In my defense, I thought the other officers might back me on this one. But for some strange reason, no one else cared to tell *Commissioner* Halbert that he was a disgrace to his uniform...

And I wonder why cops hate me?

Speaking of BBQ, all this superhero work had me *hungry*. The sun was flying directly overhead. Maybe it was best to pass on the hoards of ticked-off shields and their crying children to see what I could scrounge up for some lunch?

Regardless of what was best, I took off to see what I could scrounge up for lunch.

There's this hotdog cart down by New Wall Street, *Frank's Franks*. The man is a genius! I dare not ask what is in it, but when you order one of those bad boys fully-loaded, you get your $4.86's worth. And I'm not just saying that because he paid me to say that! I'm saying that because now and then he'll slip a homeless person a free fully-loaded on the side just to spread the word for him. We do. We fucking do!

I landed in front of Frank's cart. Rush hour, so he'd built himself quite a line. The dogs were well worth the wait. I stood there for about six minutes with my wings out. No one left the line. But everyone trying to join us kept muttering something about "pollo diablo" and took off in the opposite direction. Personally, I think that's an insult to Frank's Franks. Nothing demonic about them.

"Hey Frank," I called when I got to the front of the line. "Got any special rates for a hungry superhero?" If my mouth watered any more, the cab drivers on the road next to us would have to turn in their taxies for canoes.

"Sure do," he said. His back was turned to me while he messed with his frier. "Six bucks for a fully loaded. Seven and you'll get a side coleslaw."

"No fair!" I cried out. "It says on the sign, '$4.86.'"

"You asked if I had special rates for superheroes." He turned around to give me a wide grin that froze on his face. I'm still not sure what he saw that was more frightening, my wings or the empty line. But I'm pretty sure he only saw one of those things and completely disregarded the other. He didn't say anything though. Just kept looking right past me with that worried grin plastered on him.

God as my witness, I was going to pay him the full seven bucks! My stomach growled loud enough to shake monkeys out of treetops. And I *wanted* that coleslaw. I reached into my pockets to pull out my wallet when I made a terrible discovery.

I left my wallet in my other pants.

"Ah... Sorry, Frank, I'm going to have to catch you next time," I said over the sounds of my protesting stomach.

"Yeah. Just have… to… next time."

I flew away.

I went on autopilot for a little while. One of the perks of having wings is that there's always an empty ledge on a rooftop to sit on. As long as I looked towards the horizon instead of straight down… it wasn't too bad.

There wasn't a crime to be had for me. The sun was starting its way down the sky, but I hadn't found so much as a vagrant… except for myself. I guess I thought my debut would be a bit more… *dramatic:* car chases and purse-snatchers, women swooning after seeing me fly in and save the day, perhaps something along the line of "You're my hero, Stranger." Yeah… That would've been nice.

I have freakin *wings*. Surely *somebody* besides me thinks that's cool as hell! But it seems like I spent my day running around in big circles. Moreover, I missed a perfectly good day for begging… what has my life come to that I was more concerned about begging for eating money than I was about having my big damn hero moment?

Nobody was in any danger. All I had to do was sit back and enjoy the view. The blue sky was just right for a portrait. A few wisps of clouds chugged lazily at the edges of my vision. Bright, shining buildings reached up from the dingy streets to bask in the glamor. Any artist would be jealous to have the sight that lay casually before me.

But I felt uneasy.

I was too laid back. Too above it all. Moreover, I was greener than grass. I want to protect people. My wings are the perfect tool for that! … But a tool is only as good as the user.

I thought about DinoHyde and Hotshot Lagoon. They at least had a plan. I was just… *winging* it. I wonder if they'd let me tag along as a sidekick for a while…?

No sooner had the thought popped into my mind than I heard several helicopters take off into the air.

Something big was finally happening.

Chapter Sixteen

Let me tell you about helicopters. They're big, slow, noisy, and they've got to be the single worst method of transportation ever invented! Give me a train any day. Did you know helicopters have a strict weight limit? It's true! You can only fit about twenty people into one of them. Try to make it twenty-one and they can't even get off the ground.

The worst part? Gunmen. Dear God, the gunmen. Whoever thought it was a good idea to put sniper rifles and a Gatling gun on a giant, bulbous box with not two, but *four* rotating blades of terror—each kicking up winds of up to seventy-four kph—should be F-I-R-E-D. But it's okay! The guns make up for the strong wind by being powerful enough to shoot through three inches of steel! I'm sure *absolutely nothing* can go wrong with this design…

This, unfortunately, is the SBA-24 "Sabala" police helicopter. When one of these things takes off, you know something bad has happened. When New American criminals tried to invade Briar city, they sent *one* Sabala to quell the insurrection. When Cutter hijacked the mayor's tower, the sky roared from the five Sabala's sent to hunt him down. When a Sabala takes to the skies, the cops have gone to war.

Fourteen Sabala helicopters lifted off around the city all at once.

The wind alone blasted across my empty rooftop like a wild tornado—my senses completely overloaded! The helicopters all took up positions over the Heap, sending the Heap's Welcome wafting across the city proper for the first time in years. People keeled over.

I couldn't even *begin* to guess what was going on. Was it war? Another gang? Space aliens?? There was not a scenario in my mind that could be so bad as to justify using *fourteen* of the strongest, most lethal helicopters ever made.

On the ground, cops started waving people off the streets. SWAT vans and military jeeps rolled their way steadily past police checkpoints, along with one massive tank.

Whatever was going on in the Heap was way beyond my paygrade.

So, naturally, I threw caution to the wind and dived in headfirst.

The wind was blinding. I could feel the currents thrashing like a snake with its head cut off. The haphazard buildings were never made to resist wind pressure like this—more than a few hovels collapsed. Shots resounded through the air, followed by screams.

I started towards those nearest to me, but more shots rang out from deeper in the Heap. A swarm of SmashStone "bricks" blocked off a whole street, shouting profanities at the invading special forces. Cops in riot shields stepped forward. The gangsters started booing and throwing debris.

I was not in good shape. Ever since I entered the Heap, flying felt more like crawling. Every few seconds a powerful updraft would worm its way across, sending me into trees or a downdraft would threaten to smear me into the pavement.

Tensions rose as the cops ignored the ruffians. I don't know who fired first. But chaos erupted immediately. Some bricks started tearing up the town… literally. Rock addicts: They could lift compact cars if they got pissed enough. But it comes at a wicked cost. One girl in the crowd started pulling up a streetlamp like it was a carrot. The cops shot her over and over. I could see the blood-sprays. But that didn't stop her from pulling the light straight out of the concrete and hurling it right into the middle of the cops. She died almost immediately afterward. The drugs may give a person superstrength for a hot minute, but *nothing* lets you come back from six shots in the chest.

I tucked my wings in close. The change in aerodynamics hurtled me straight into the middle of the chaos.

Not that it helped much. I thought that I could subdue the thugs before the cops brought out the big guns and eradicate them all. Things didn't turn out as well as I hoped. I was able to knock out a few thugs before they turned on me, but the cops kept firing indiscriminately.

Someone nearby screamed. It was a kid.

Immediately, I turned my back on the riot to save the kid. I started this whole mess to save children; I wasn't about to let one down now! I caught a glass bottle over the back of my head for my trouble. The kid was cowering behind a concrete stairway. I scooped him up in one arm and ran him to a building where people were hastily boarding up doors and windows. They opened up just a hair, eager arms gesturing for me to get inside. Wordlessly, I stuffed the kid through the doorway and continued running off down the street.

I could've kicked myself that my first instinct was to try and stop the war. That was naive. And yet...

No more kids in caskets, I reminded myself. *Catch the people.*

I turned a corner and ran head-first into another patrol of cops. These guys didn't appear to be fighting anyone, but, the second I approached, they all started drawing guns and firing. If my wings weren't bulletproof, I'd be paste… again. The force pushed me backward. At the same time, the wind pulled me forwards. The cops kept shouting unintelligibly at me. I figured it was only a matter of time before one of those bullets found their way past my wings. Another updraft stormed through the road; I caught it, and the wind shot me a block and a half before I touched the ground again.

I tucked into a back alley and immediately ran into yet another cop. I recognized him as the same guy I met on the rooftop back before I intervened in the bank heist. What a small world.

"Ah! Pollo Diablo!!" He shouted. This time he was equipped with his sidearm and he started unloading every shot in the gun at me. I just barely managed to avoid getting a chest full of holes by tucking back out the ally the same way I came in. Looks like I made a friend on the police force… yay…

Everywhere I turned it was police marching or gang members "protesting." I kept driving deeper and deeper into the Heap. The heart of the conflict had to be there.

I passed by another small alleyway right as another squad of cops popped out of it.

"Pollo Diablo spotted on West Young street." The commander shouted into his comms unit. "Open fire, open fire!"

I had no other choice but to return to the skies… such as it was. The strong winds blew me well out of range of the ground troops, but there was no way I'd be able to help anyone on the ground.

I zoomed through the remaining buildings, trying desperately to stay in the currents that took me where I wanted to go. I only spilled out of the slipstream and slammed into a building once… Okay, twice.

The center of the Heap is a small clearing. Once upon a time, it was a city block just like any other, but after the Great Corporate War, several businesses had been demolished. Rather than re-building, the citizens voted to level the block and renovate it as a public space. Sidewalks and shrubbery with absolutely no cars in sight… until today.

Swat vans circled the entire square like an angry black wall. This place was the farthest spot in the Heap from the helicopters. I could see clearly without needing to cover my face. I could also hear! From the moment I landed, I could hear the cops cocking their guns in anticipation of a fight.

The ground started shaking. From one of the sides, the vans parted to let in the tank I saw from before. I squinted across the field as best I could. Whatever the cops were after, this had to be it. But there was no-one else in sight.

From every direction, cops had their guns drawn and aimed right down the center of the square. But I couldn't figure out who they were aiming at.

Then, the tank trained its cannon on one target. Me.

Chapter Seventeen

Have you ever wondered what it's like to get shot at by a tank? Probably not, but I'll tell you anyway. It's terrifying! *No duh*, right? It starts in your eyes. The cannon lines up to your face, and it looks impossibly large. The muzzle looks bigger than anything you could imagine. And it dawns on you… *there's no way it could possibly miss.*

You think to move… but your body *won't*. Your wings fall back, your arms go slack… How long have you stood there? One second feels like a lifetime. You might not have any more.

…

And then. There's a… *snap*. Your brain kicks in and desperately tries to think of a way out—There's no time! One thought surfaces. You find yourself speaking it out loud.

"Oh… Shi—"

My whole world exploded. The impossible happened. *It missed.* But when we're talking about munitions larger than 120mm, a near miss is close enough.

The ground dropped away from my feet. Fire and shell fragments scattered in every direction. I was lucky. Very, *very* lucky. The shell detonated behind me and to the side—if it had landed even one foot closer, it would've killed me. I could feel the fragments that missed me shoot by like a flock of birds. My wings caught the rest. I lost several feathers. For the first time since I discovered them, my wings were bleeding. I knew now that my wings were not invulnerable. If that shell had hit me directly, I would've died. Even if I caught the shell with my wings.

I was desperate to not get caught by another blast. I took to the sky even though every flap ached. The cyclone of air currents battered me hither and yon. I couldn't fight them. With so many feathers out, I could barely take flight, let alone keep myself steady. I felt like I was on a harness that would drop me to the ground at any second.

I blew past a building. The Dwight building of all places…

In front of me, a police helicopter pulled forward to block my path. This was a nightmare. The buildings were too close together! If we were on a level area, I could fly circles around the chopper blindfolded. But here, the shiny, red-white-and-blue helicopters didn't have to worry about that. And their way of flight carried one significant advantage: They could rise and fall faster than I could.

Trying to go over or under them would be suicide. The pressure vacuum alone would force me onto those blades and turn my beautiful sepia body into a fine scarlet mist.

I flung myself out of the air current into the only direction available to me: an alleyway that had a bunch of dead air. A shot rang out. A burning hot line gouged its way into the side of my neck.

Snipers, I thought. *Of course there are snipers in the helicopters.*

I took off again, flying as fast as I was able.

Flying is a bit like swimming. If you keep flapping your wings, you'll exhaust yourself. You have to switch it up, glide a little. Dive for a quick second. You can't just keep powering your way through…

I had to keep powering my way through the gale. There was no time to stop! Up until this point, I was running on adrenaline alone. Now, I was flying on fumes… My wings felt like they'd been carrying a two hundred pound man through the air all day. Which they had.

Moreover, I was still a new flyer. This was the hardest workout I'd ever had with my wings. Plus, I could tell I'd lost a lot of blood from the shell fragments.

But the nightmare wasn't over.

In front of me, another helicopter slotted into place. Another shot rebounded off my wings, causing me to nearly spiral out of control into the ground where a veritable army of cops waited with more guns and handcuffs.

I zipped higher and folded over a building to escape the line of fire. But almost immediately, the first helicopter closed into the gap behind me, forcing me onward and into another current.

I caught the current until it spilled out into another killbox with yet another helicopter. It felt like a game of chess. The helicopters were being coordinated against me. They were moving in a way that cut off all my options of escape and forced the currents to box me in tighter and tighter. There was a malevolence to this stratagem. Whoever was behind all this enjoyed watching me suffer.

Again and again, I'd duck into an alleyway just to have the end blocked off. I'd try to skip over the buildings just to find one of the choppers waiting with their deadly blades whirring mere inches away from my hide.

I was being directed like a flock of sheep. Herded through the twisting paths to one destination. A clear building. I was at the end of my rope. My wings could barely flap anymore, I was being held in the air by something a little less substantial than a prayer.

I tumbled onto the building, the last of my strength used up.

Time to meet my puppetmaster, I thought as I stumbled to my feet.

Around me from all sides, police helicopters rose up above the skyline in a spectacular display. I could *feel* the snipers all aiming. From within the bellies of the choppers, assault troops dropped down. Each armed with RPG's. Like my day wasn't bad enough.

I was surrounded.

Chapter Eighteen

"I knew I should've grabbed a few smoke bombs," I grumbled to myself. One of the officers stepped forward and fired his RPG. I braced myself for the hit. All I could do was pray my feathers could deflect the explosives.

They didn't.

The blast ripped my feathers off all along my right wing. I collapsed and shrieked at the top of my lungs. I hurriedly withdrew the meaty part of my wing into my back. I didn't know if that would help, but it was the only option I had. My wing went from feeling like it was on fire (probably because it was), to a dull throbbing somewhere in my back.

A man stepped forward calmly. "All units: hold your fire. The subject's down. Keep a line of sight, but *only* open fire if he tries to fly away."

The Catcher. I found it hard to believe he was the one behind all this. To mobilize so many officers, he'd need way more pull than even a special agent of the FBI could manage.

"You didn't have to go through all this trouble for me. I would've come all this way for a purse-snatcher."

"Or one of Frank's franks?"

"You know damn well they're the best franks in the city!" I protested. There wasn't much else I could do. I tried to get back to my feet, but I was exhausted. I collapsed on my back and let the humiliation wash over me. The Catcher took my wings away. I might never fly again… The thought alone made my body feel like it was lined with lead. "Just take me in already."

The Catcher stood over me triumphantly. "What's the matter, *devil chicken*? Job too hard for ya?"

"All things being even, I think I preferred 'the pigeon' as a nickname."

The Catcher made a face. "Yeah, I didn't really pick *pollo diablo*. The satellite repair man you terrorized earlier didn't speak English all that well. The media really ate up his description of you and they ran with *his* name instead of mine."

"How terrible… you should sue."

"Shut it, *convict*. You're under arrest. We'll get to the list of charges once they stop coming in. I'm impressed, it's a pretty exhaustive list for one day. Maybe even a record."

"I thought I was doing alright."

"Is it true you called the Police chief an 'irresponsible fat lard of criminal corruption?'"

I didn't answer him. Thank God I had a mask on; otherwise, the Catcher would've seen just how embarrassed I was. He ratcheted one cuff on my arm, flipped me over, and ratcheted the second.

That was it. Whatever happened next was completely out of my hands… once again, I wasn't in control of my fate… not that I was doing that good of a job to begin with.

The Catcher forced me to my feet and frog-marched me to the stairwell. The helicopters didn't leave. No doubt they had orders to keep watch over me all the way to the jail cell. I couldn't see any sniper dot's on me… but I could feel them. Every step I took, someone tensed up.

But that someone was not Randel Dregg. No, the Catcher sounded mighty pleased with himself. He ordered the ground troops to start cleanup operations, processing gang members and other civilians who protested the Heap being used as one gigantic trap.

"So, what's your name, bird breath?" he asked me after a few steps.

I didn't answer.

The Catcher kept pressing, "Don't talk if you want. We have your feather, remember? As we speak, your DNA is being analyzed and run through every database in the book. It's only a matter of time before we know the whole truth about you."

"You wouldn't believe me if I told you," I grumbled.

"Try me," he dared.

"Well… okay, I'll tell you." I leaned in close and whispered, "I'm secretly a space alien sent to earth to test your limits so others of my race can conquer you all."

The Catcher harrumphed in disappointment and gave me a rough shove for my efforts. "I've seen that movie," he complained. "It wasn't very good."

"The book was better."

From behind us, there was a commotion. Officers drew their weapons and fired. The Catcher clamped his arm around my throat and his gun to my head. Using me as a shield, he twisted until we were walking backward to the stairwell.

"What kind of stunt are you pulling now?"

I shrugged. "I don't know," I said honestly, "This isn't my doing at all."

More shouting, more shooting. The Catcher tightened his grip. "If it's not you, then who is it?"

"I said, 'I don't know!'" I protested. "I'm a space alien, remember? It's not like I have any friends."

"I don't know what you've got planned, but it won't work. Any sign of movement and I'll—"

Before the Catcher could say *exactly* what he planned to do with me, a big, bright chunk of blue metal bounced off the concrete right in front of us and slammed into my chest, knocking the air out of my lungs.

It beeped. The Catcher kicked me over. I rolled off it right as the metal device went off. He thought it was a bomb… I thought it was a bomb. It wasn't.

The device let off a flash of blue light that washed over everything on or near the roof. I managed to jam my eyes shut before the worst of it, but the Catcher took it all to the face. He flailed wildly and fell to the floor even as I was getting back to my feet.

I had hope! My story wasn't over just yet.

I stood up tall in just enough time to witness the fourteen Sabala police helicopters lose altitude. More people shouted. Cops on the sidelines tried to fire their RPG's, only to fail.

And… I hesitated. If my wing was still injured, would I even be able to pull it out now? Let alone fly with it… But, without my wings, I didn't know where to go or what to do to escape!

In front of me, a figure leaped up from below. Gunshots rang out as the cops frantically fought off this new assailant. But he cut through them ruthlessly, sending some flying back with a single punch.

I started to run, but then the figure's tail snapped and sent another cop flying. *I recognized that tail.* DinoHyde rushed to my side and let out a blast of fire around us from his maw. The only thing that contained my excitement was that all my words got tangled up in my throat.

I made some unintelligible grunts and DinoHyde—without skipping a beat—reached one arm around my chest and his tail around my feet. I was being manhandled like a piece of luggage! DinoHyde took off running to the nearest ledge. Bullets zinged randomly overhead as cops fired wildly into the flames. DinoHyde didn't stop at the ledge. He jumped straight off the roof and we fell forty stories straight down.

I blacked out before we hit the bottom.

Chapter Nineteen

I didn't want to dream. But I didn't have a choice.

I was falling. The floors of the building rushed past me. The ground leaped up to embrace me. I hit the ground. Funny, there wasn't much pain. My body felt heavy against the pavement. This was death.

I died.

But I… wasn't dead? Or was I? I had wings. Why didn't I use them to fly?

Right… The Catcher shot them off with an RPG…

I laughed. Wings? RPG's?? How absurd! Dying on the pavement was much more realistic. At least Death was kind.

…

Wait…

Death *was* kind. There it was now. Standing over me, cloak billowing in the nonexistent wind. The rain, which had been falling so quickly, now stood frozen in its fall. Forever falling. Such is the power of Death. I could continue to fall eternally. But Death spared me that fate. It let me hit the pavement.

Thank you, I tried to tell it.

Death turned to me. The skeletal grin loomed over me. Its empty eye sockets bored into mine, and I saw my own soul reflected in its blackness. But Death wasn't happy. Death was sad. I guess even in death I wasn't living up to my potential. Death pointed a finger at the sky. *Look,* it seemed to say.

I was falling again. The ground leaped up to embrace me. But I did not hit the ground. I kept falling. Lightning flashed, and the city shined with its blue light. Then I remembered; I wasn't falling at all. It was the city, a raindrop caught forever in freefall.

Catch it, a voice begged me… Silly voice. It didn't even have to ask. I had already reached out my hands. I had to catch the city before it fell. The voice was irrelevant.

My hands caught the ground, and I died again.

Death stood over my corpse. *You cannot catch it.* It seemed to say. *Death is all that awaits you.*

But I didn't care. Not really. Death was so much easier than flying. Easier than being a raindrop frozen forever. I had to finish falling eventually.

But I could catch the city before I left… I could…

I looked into Death's hollow sockets. Its face was completely unreadable. Whatever thoughts or observations the Grim Reaper held, whether good or bad, remained a mystery to my broken corpse.

I woke up with a start.

"Easy, *easy* man," a strange voice said. A firm hand on my shoulder pushed me back against a table. It was smooth and cold. Metal. That was all I could tell since my vision was completely obscured. "You've just been through Hell and back," The voice continued, "the last thing you need is to pull a muscle."

"Why can't I see?" I asked.

"I turned your ski mask around. I had to take off my helmet to finish this. You can put it back on straight if you want—I'm back in costume already."

This voice… it was familiar. But not… I couldn't put my finger on it, but it sounded like someone I'd met before.

"I… The last thing I remember was DinoHyde—"

"Yeah, that was quite a jump! I wrenched a few servos loose in that fall, but I'll have it fixed up before tonight."

So, this man was DinoHyde… I twisted my mask around as he suggested, but immediately regretted that decision. The room we were in was pure white, with white walls, and bright white fluorescent lights. *Oof.* The sheer brilliance of it all was enough to make me recoil so hard I nearly fell off the table.

"I'm surprised you're going out there in an old ski mask," DinoHyde continued. His voice sounded… rough. Jagged, like a piece of rusted metal… And a bit on the deeper end of the spectrum. I got the impression that he wasn't as young as I'd first assumed him to be. With a voice like that, he had to be pushing fifty… at least.

Not that I could tell by looking at him. Now that my vision had returned, I could see him leaning back against a worktable, his tail flickering contentedly behind his feet.

Before, he'd always stayed out of my sight, only showing himself in half lighting or extreme circumstances. It made it hard for me to see him fully. Now, I could see that he was clearly in a costume. The "scales" on his arm were sewn together with crude stitches on par with my own. And his "mouth" was clearly a false head — complete with fake eyes that lit up. A dark visor and a smooth metal plate covered his real head as it poked out from the throat. If I stared at a certain angle, it looked like DinoHyde was trying to swallow a motorcycle helmet.

It was quite an elaborate cowl. My failed attempt was embarrassingly simple by comparison. "Yeah, well… I suck at sewing," I told him honestly. "I would've loved to have a bird-shaped head, but I couldn't make that look good."

"Is that so?" he asked. His voice was calm, but his tail betrayed his eagerness, swishing even faster across the floor. "I may have something you'd be interested in." From behind him, DinoHyde pulled out a gorgeous cowl shaped elegantly into exactly the kind of hawk's head that I'd been so crudely trying to replicate. And the eyes were perfectly placed! If I didn't know any better, I'd have assumed he'd just handed me a jawless, extra-large hawk head.

"This is a prototype armored head I'd been working on for a flying version of the DinoHyde suit. I couldn't ever get the wings to work right, so I scrapped the project — but I always lamented that this design would go to waste."

"You're not just giving this to me?" I asked incredulously.

"… kinda," DinoHyde replied. "There's one catch."

"Let's hear it."

"You have to be my apprentice."

I paused for a full minute; *I swear*! Too much was happening too fast. I'm not sure *exactly* how long it took me to respond, but I'm pretty sure I mumbled, "You're kidding, right?" because DinoHyde adopted a really disappointed pose. I felt bad immediately, but after months of chasing this myth, just hoping for a chance to explain myself, he turns up out of the blue and offers me the gig! Part of me wasn't even sure that I was fully awake.

"I've been looking for an apprentice for… a long time," DinoHyde said. "You're the first newbie to show in over twenty years with enough talent to warrant it."

"Um… are we talking about the same me? I wouldn't exactly call what I have talent."

DinoHyde didn't laugh. He passed the cowl to me with a perfect toss. Naturally, I caught it out of the air reflexively. The one time a fumble would've actually been in my favor. DinoHyde turned around and led me to a worktable filled with newspaper clippings. "I've been reading up on you. Dressed as a hobo, you jumped into the bank heist a month ago without even flinching at the danger. Ten minutes later, you blast through the window carrying the only two wounded hostages who couldn't leave on their own."

I mean… when he put it *like that*, it *did* seem kinda heroic.

"And last night, even though it was clearly a trap to ground you for good, you selflessly rushed into the Heap to protect the civilians."

My face burned so much from embarrassment, I'm surprised my ski mask didn't catch fire.

DinoHyde, his back to me, saw nothing of my shame. Instead, he continued, "It's a rough game, being a vigilante. But if you survived last night, you can survive anything. All you need is a little time… and guidance."

"Well… I *definitely* need guidance," I told him. It was the only thing he'd said so far that I agreed with.

"Then you'll do it? You'll be my apprentice?" DinoHyde turned back to face me. His tail swishing eagerly behind him.

"I-I guess." It's not like I had anything better to do.

"Good," he agreed gruffly. Gesturing around, DinoHyde walked on the other side of the table I had been laying on. I, meanwhile, did another double-take.

The light, as bright as it had been, blinded me before I got a good look at the place. As such, I hadn't really taken the time to look around much. The room was almost twice the size of the space I'd been seeing.

Right smack-dab in the center was the chassis of a Sabala Police Helicopter, all sawed up and welded back together. Bits and pieces of it were strewn around the room, hung up on various machines, or straight up disassembled on a bunch of rolling tables.

One wall was lined with row after row of boxed shelves, probably carrying all kinds of bolts, sprockets, and tools. A few doors dotted around here and there. On the far wall was a bunch of computer monitors displaying all sorts of images that I vaguely recognized as blueprints—one of which was for the Sabala in the center of the room.

I'd missed all of that talking with DinoHyde. *Rule one, always check the surroundings*, I told myself.

"First things first," DinoHyde intoned, deftly navigating the chaotic workshop. "We need to hide your identity and make sure the police can't find anything useful about your gear." He glanced back at me still holding the Hawkhead cowl and staring dumbfounded at the surroundings. "You might also want to put that on. The high-res images are disorienting sometimes. The sooner you get used to it, the better. Just don't let me see your face. If I get caught, I don't want to have to turn you in." He said with a look so pointed, I got the message immediately. No more questions about his identity.

He turned back away again and I quickly switched masks. It didn't just cover my face, it dropped down completely over the back of my head. The back slotted down over my collar with some kind of cloth on the inside so my head wasn't touching any metal. The front came down to the tip of my nose. The soft memory foam molded itself to the exact shape of my cheekbones. The metal beak dipped down to about my jawline. If I bent my head down far enough, I could touch it to my chest, but only just barely.

For a second, I couldn't see anything. But then the second passed and the screen flashed on in front of me. It was a High Definition, VR micro-screen. And I could tell from the images the camera was made from not one, but two Oculus Eye Lenses.

My jaw popped as I looked around the room in wonder. Seeing things through this cowl was like looking at the world through the eyes of a bird. From where I stood, I could see the welding lines on the Sabala. I could see a screw poking out from a shelf, and I could count how many spirals it had. Then, with a blink, the room zoomed out and I was looking through normal eyes again. All as quick as thought.

"Woah," I exclaimed rather anti-climatically.

"It's a lot to take in, isn't it?" DinoHyde laughed. "The cameras are actually on the sides of the mask and can be pointed independently of each other. If you're not careful, you could go cross-eyed."

A quick little experiment of my own proved his words true, but I found that if I closed one eye or the other I could switch cameras easily enough without any headaches.

"I based it off the same tech in my suits," DinoHyde bragged. "You'll have infrared, ultraviolet, night vision, X-ray vision, voice analysis… I even stuffed in a voice modulator."

As he talked, menu options popped up on my HUD. I only just managed to tap the voice modulator and select the default option before it and every other option disappeared. They were probably keyed to DinoHyde's voice. I'd have to talk to him about that.

"How did you even *do* all of this?" I asked incredulously. Then, at the sound of my own voice through the modulator, I started cackling. The modulator sounded just like a hawk! Or, at the very least, what I imagined a hawk-human hybrid would sound like.

DinoHyde, to his credit, waited patiently for me to quit playing around before explaining. "My real identity lets me be a bit sticky-fingered with Barron Corp technologies. They've noticed pieces of their tec disappearing for years, and correctly blamed me, DinoHyde, for the thefts."

"That's how the rumor that you haunt Barron Corp warehouses got started!" I guessed excitedly. Just happy to have noticed something relevant, for once.

"Yeah… I also invented half of their computers back in the day. My R-MIG computer chip would've revolutionized how technology works for people if Barron himself hadn't shut down the project."

I didn't even have to ask. DinoHyde took one look at my puzzled face and knew to continue. "Random Motion Impulse Generator-It's a chip of my own design. It reads basic brainwaves to predict what the user will need it to do and then *does* it. I made it so humans could interface easier with computers. But, when I built my suit I found it had… *other* applications. The 'eyes' of your cowl are actually electronically generated by the R-MIG to look like real bird eyes. My tail works the same way." The tail lifted up from behind DinoHyde and gave a little wave to demonstrate.

Something clicked in my mind, and as usual, came out of my mouth immediately. "I can express emotion through my cowl!"

"Yes. Your cowl looks like a real face. Albeit, one that can't possibly be real in nature."

"That's incredible!" I gushed. "That's mind-blowing, and fantastic, a-and-"

"It's nothing compared to my other tricks."

"There's more?" I said. The disbelief on my face brought a chuckle out of DinoHyde's stoic demeanor.

"Of course there's more, weren't you listening? We still have to hack the BCPD and erase all traces of your real identity."

And like that, I was ready to bolt. "You can't just… *hack* the BCDP!" I hissed through gritted teeth. The voice modulator changed my hiss into an irritated squawk. After the cops and the military fused into one entity, their security system was absolute. They had backups for their backups, every detection system known to man, and a few we still hadn't discovered yet… it was impossible. Countless hackers had tried and failed, only to have their location revealed and every camera, mic, and smart-fridge track them until the cops could arrive.

"I already did," DinoHyde said, brushing off my protests. He tapped a few buttons on the computer next to him and my police file popped up on its screen. "This is your DNA profile. The Catcher must've found some blood or hair to get such a clear sample. It's being sent out to find a correct match. This gives us a small window of opportunity. We're going to give you a whole new identity."

He pulled out a card from a drawer. "This is the DNA sample from Mark Deviss. He's a veteran who died in El Salvador. His profile matches what the police already know about you. Black, five-foot-four, twenty to forty years of age, and disappeared under mysterious circumstances. Get this, he was a bomber pilot. It's the perfect cover."

"How do you know I'm not Mark Deviss?"

This question did not phase DinoHyde in the slightest. "You're too young, for one thing. You're in your mid-to-late twenties, Mark would be thirty-six if he was still alive. And for another thing, I witnessed Mark's death firsthand."

My shocked expression must've been really obvious because DinoHyde didn't even wait for me to ask, and continued, "Mark was a vigilante I worked with back in the day. We faked his death together and… Let's just leave it at that. He's dead now, and his name is a perfect fit for your cover. That leaves your *real* identity for yourself. It'll take the police years to catch on… if they ever do."

DinoHyde popped open a second window with Mark's DNA profile on it. A few clicks of the mouse later and the two DNA samples were seamlessly swapped.

"Won't there be like… some kind of record that these pages were hacked?"

"There would be," DinoHyde grumbled, "if this was an ordinary computer. Let's just say a perk of my secret identity was that I was on the ground floor when the BCPD was being built. I was able to secretly add an extra computer to floor sixteen on the physical lines, but covered it up on the paperwork.

"Between this and the policy to keep server data all air-gapped from outside sources, the BCPD are just not prepared for this kind of hacking. All the user's data is kept on the computer that does it; this computer. And, of course, this computer is completely air-gapped from the other servers in this room. If I want to transfer files, I have to physically download a copy and walk it to the other computers."

I'd been nodding like I understood what was going on, but now DinoHyde was looking at me like he expected a reaction. I shook my head. "So, what does that mean in English?"

"It means there's no record that I hacked these pages. As far as they know, *they weren't hacked.* Just another computer clerk clearing up a discrepancy in the paperwork."

DinoHyde went back to scrolling through my file. His tail tapped anxiously against the floor. Sure enough, a second later he looked up and announced, "we have a problem." I asked what it was, and he pointed to the evidence file. "I can't find what happened to your wings anywhere here. It looks like the Catcher is breaking the rules and keeping the evidence off-site. This isn't good. If he suspects the BCPD server's been compromised..."

"I don't think that's it," I assured him. "He blasted my wings off with an RPG last night, just before you showed up. It wouldn't be in the report because I don't think he knows what happened either."

"Ouch," DinoHyde winced. "That's gotta hurt. I could help you rebuild if you like. If you've got the blueprints-"

"No need. I just need to focus for a second. I've never done this with them so badly damaged before." I stood back and imagined stretching my wings out from my back. My right wing did *not* want to stretch out! The left one came out fine, but moving the right wing was like moving a broken arm; *it hurt!* I fell to my knees and cradled the wing as best I could with my right arm.

"My God," DinoHyde exclaimed, jumping back against the computer. "They're real!"

"Of course they're real," I gasped between waves of agony. "Do you really think an idiot like me could invent something like this?"

"Real…" DinoHyde mumbled, his body frozen in an absurd position. "They're… real… … Wings… real…"

"Hey man, snap out of it," I said, snapping my fingers under his helmet to get his attention. "You're the vigilante superhero, remember? You're supposed to be used to this sort of thing."

DinoHyde turned his head slowly to me. He let out a bubble of genuine laughter. Which turned into a stream of laughs. Like, *maniacal* laughs. God, that was *terrifying*. I thought I'd broken him for good, but he stopped… eventually. He put his arm on my left shoulder and said, "I don't think anyone could be prepared to expect you, *Pollo Diablo*."

"About that, can I change my nickname?"

"No."

Chapter Twenty

"One: Make a plan; stick to the plan.

Two: Never let them see you coming.

Three: Hit fast, *and* hard.

Four: Beat your enemies in one move.

Five: Never speak; always intimidate.

Six: Never get caught.

Seven: Never—"

"Wait—what was number three again?" I asked. DinoHyde and I were "sparing." What that means is I was getting hit every time he spouted off a rule. I'd win if I could dodge him without using my wings.

I was losing.

DinoHyde flipped and his tail lashed itself across my face like a whip. I collapsed like a sack of potatoes and bled all over his shiny white floor. "Never bleed," he finished, offering me his hand. "You *have* to be vigilant. A hero only bleeds when he's messed everything up. You only get one shot in the real world. You mess up; you bleed. You bleed; you die."

"That sounds a bit harsh, doesn't it?"

"*Life* is harsh. People live, bleed, and die. Heroes don't have that luxury. We have to keep fighting; have to keep winning. A hero has to be a symbol—has to be larger than life. A single drop of blood could mean the end if you're not careful."

"I'll be careful," I promised.

"Not good enough. Your fighting style is beyond incompetent. If you go out into the field like this, you'll die."

"I'd do a hell of a lot better if you let me fight with my wings," I squawked indignantly.

"Flying around the battlefield is not fighting."

"No, I mean for hitting back," I insisted. "My wings are stronger and tougher than my arms. They're longer and faster too. When I was making my suit, I played around with them for practice sometimes."

DinoHyde glowered at me skeptically. I didn't even know such a feat was possible. But after spending time with the vigilante, I was coming to learn that he'd mastered the art of mixing every possible expression into his fierce grimace. After sparing with him for a few hours, I was getting the hang of reading his moods.

"Look, just let me try," I pleaded. "I'll show you what I'm made of."

"Irrelevant. Your wings have already been blasted off once, what will you do when it happens again? Without your wings, you have nothing to fall back on."

"You don't get to say that to me until you get out of that suit and kick my ass."

"Fine," he said, the chill in his voice ran straight through any certainty I had that provoking him was a good idea. "Come at me with everything you've got. And I'll do the same."

He didn't look the type to play around with rule #3, so I blasted my wings out and immediately launched into an offensive barrage. Using my wings, I flipped up and over him, lashing out with my wingtips at the back of his head.

DinoHyde saw through the attack, however, and clamped his iron hands over my exposed feathers.

Instinctively, I pulled my wings as far apart as I could. This did two things: The first was it caused DinoHyde's arms to spark as several of his servomechanisms exceeded their maximum capacity. The other thing that happened is I got pulled down on his back. I tried to kick, but it was like hitting a steel wall. The impact ran up my coiled legs, and I bounced harmlessly off the vigilante.

For a single instant, I thought I was safe from a counter-attack, then DinoHyde made a powerful leap and lashed his tail across my head. The hit knocked me right out of the air.

"I see what you mean now," the vigilante said. His arms hung awkwardly as everything past the elbows was effectively dead weight without those servos. "But it's still not good enough. People will only ever be surprised by something *once*. Then they adapt. They plan and prepare new tactics. If all you've got is the one move, they'll tear you up."

"Then I'll just have to make new moves, won't I?"

DinoHyde smiled at that… well, his tail flicked approvingly while his body stance became less aggressive. I took that to be a smile, whether one actually graces his lips or not was a secret no-one could know thanks to his cowl.

"Come on," he said, offering his tail as a hand. "There's something I want to check out."

"The way you flew just now felt… off. I can't say why. But it's clear your wings have more muscles in them than your arms. The servos I employ have been rigorously tested, they're capable of withstanding up to half a ton of pressure. Do you know what that means?"

I thought about the question, but I never really had a head for science. "My wings are really strong?" I guessed.

I could *feel* the eye-roll coming off of DinoHyde. He sighed and sat down at a workbench. Although his forearms were useless, his fingers still worked fine. He picked up a long screwdriver and started making adjustments to his forearm. "It means you've shown me two impossible things today. Real wings, and unreal force. For the first time in fifty years, I'm at a loss to explain what's going on. The world was much simpler when it was just men in uniforms fighting each other endlessly."

"You're talking about the Great Corporate War," I realized.

DinoHyde nodded, not taking his eyes off his arm. "Everything was black and white back then. Good or Bad, Right or Wrong, With the people or Against them. Now Cutter and his gang rule half the city, while Smastone has all but taken over what's left of downtown… The Heap."

"The gangs are why the Heap is as trashed up as it is." I jumped in.

DinoHyde looked up with a scoff. "The gangs aren't the problem, they're the symptoms."

"I don't follow."

DinoHyde sighed and put down his screwdriver. "The gangs exist because of bad politics," he explained. "It's no coincidence that the poorest parts of the city are the same place as where the gang violence is at the highest. The city abandoned the people who needed it the most. The gangs offer an outlet for revenge and justice. They promise a better life—"

"Full of drugs and violence."

"A *better* life… not necessarily a good one," DinoHyde insisted. "Most of these gang members are just kids who don't think they have any other choice. Those that don't join… they die."

He paused for a moment. Something in his arm sparked a couple of times and he went back to talking as if nothing had happened. "I had a kid die just a few months ago. He too had promise, but unlike you, he didn't have power. He tried to wipe out both gangs in a massive shootout, but it backfired. And even if it hadn't, even if his half-baked plan had worked, by this time today we'd be right back where we are today. Just with different players."

"Y-you don't know that—you *can't* know that… not for sure," I stammered back at him. To hear myself be referenced in third-person like that shook me to the core. For one chilling heartbeat I thought he *knew* who I was and blackmailing me. But he continued.

"I lived through it," DinoHyde said without pausing. He didn't even look up from the arm. "I didn't think drug dealers got any worse than Harvey Degoul until I locked Degoul in prison and SmashStone took over." His arm sparked aggressively, causing DinoHyde to drop his screwdriver. "As I thought, you outright overloaded them. I'll have to re-route for now." He continued fiddling with his arm nonchalantly and I realized that him referencing me to myself was nothing more than one outrageous coincidence.

After he was satisfied with poking around in his arm, DinoHyde walked over to a large roll table that held the Sabala's engine. The table came up to DinoHyde's waist, and the engine was so massive a person could've crawled inside it. DinoHyde clamped his gauntlet over a large handle on the side and experimented by pushing and pulling the roll table.

I'd been standing a few feet away while DinoHyde played with his suit. I started to join him, but he waved me back towards a clear spot near the far wall. "Here rookie," he grunted. "Try catching this." With a small groan of exertion, DinoHyde whipped the roll table around him and sent it straight at me!

Like a dumbass, I tried to catch it. Word to the wise, not a good idea. My body crumpled against the table like a car. I was damn lucky I didn't just get rolled under it! The wall behind me loomed large and I knew if I didn't do something I'd be squashed flat.

I flared my wings out behind me and, though it felt like I was straining every bone in my body, I brought the table to a full stop with three feet to spare.

"Well, well," DinoHyde mused. "Now you've shown me three impossible things."

"What was that all about?" I sputtered, rubbing my shoulders that had gone stiff after catching the roll table.

"Just testing a theory," DinoHyde shot back coolly. "Now I know you truly are an impossible bird, Devil Chicken."

"Stop calling me that!" I bristled.

"It's not up to me," he shrugged. "Only the press and the Catcher come up with nicknames around here. Now follow me. Since we know that'll work, I've got another toy for you to test out."

"I'm not a guinea pig!" I complained. But DinoHyde paid me no mind. He led me across the room to what looked like a weapons testing range. There were a few training dummies a couple of feet away. At the time, I assumed that was where DinoHyde trained and tested his weapons before taking his suit into the field, but in the twenty years I've known him, I've never seen him use those facilities even once.

"Here," he said, pulling two heavy cylinders off a shelf. "See if you can lift these."

I flared my wings out in annoyance. "Not likely," I squawked. "I'm tired of being your punching bag! When you said I was going to be your apprentice, I thought you meant we'd be going on patrol, punching out bad guys, and uncovering mysteries."

"There'll be plenty of that," DinoHyde promised. "But we can't leave until nightfall anyway. I still need to repair my arms and, while we wait, you need to get a better grip on what you can and can't do. Now grab these Punchers and see if you can use them."

The feathers on my back refused to settle down; they stayed all ruffled up despite my best attempt to put on a patient face. The cylinders looked *suspiciously* like robot arms you'd see in a cartoon. One end had a three-fingered claw which balled up into a fist, the other end was hollow with a handle in it. The whole thing looked like a thick metal sleeve. DinoHyde handed me one of the cylinders and, just as I was questioning what their purpose was, I "fired" it by mistake.

The arm *punched* out a good four feet. Judging from the force of the blow, I guessed it was supposed to do something cool like punch through steel. But unfortunately, Newton's third law of motion doesn't care about cool things.

All that force snapped back at me, causing me to drop the cylinder. It nearly ripped a hole in my gut!

After that, I did my best to lift the Punchers, as DinoHyde called the cylinders, but putting in all my effort wasn't enough to raise them to my chest. The clawed ends remained firmly planted on the ground.

"That's about what I expected," DinoHyde confided, his tail swishing excitedly. "I made them to work with my suits, but they're impractical."

"Then why are you making me carry them?"

"I want you to try flying while holding them."

I didn't see what the point of this exercise was, but I knew by now that questioning DinoHyde wasn't going to get me answers that I could understand. Instead, I unfurled my wings as widely as I could stretch them, which, for the record, wasn't all that far yet (my right wing still hurt like it was full of needles!), and I lifted myself off the ground, focusing extra hard to keep myself from dropping the Punchers.

DinoHyde himself watched me impassively, with his arms folded across his chest for good measure. But his tail lost its shit! Personally, I didn't see what was so impressive, but I played along, flapping side to side when he barked orders and even managed to whip around and use one of the Punchers without dislocating my arm.

DinoHyde asked me to set down after a few minutes, and I gratefully obliged him. The Punchers were *heavy*. After only a few minutes of messing around with them, I was already sweating bullets.

"What d'you think of them?" he asked after I'd finished taking a big gulp out of a paper cup full of water he'd handed me.

"They're not bad," I admitted. "But way too heavy. I can't use them like this. My arms feel like they're about to fall off, and I can't use them if I'm not flying."

DinoHyde hummed to himself. "With a reliable weapon to fall back on, your fighting style wouldn't matter quite so much." Something on the ground caught his eye and he harrumphed amusingly. "Either way, you need some new shoes," he said pointing down to my hobo boots. The poor things were pulling apart at the seams. You could see my socks peeking through.

I started to sigh again, but DinoHyde adopted a pondering posture. "You know, I think I might be able to modify the Punchers to work with your feet. It shouldn't even be that hard. Funny, I never thought about using them as feet attachments before. There's no way to balance—but, then again, you don't have to worry about balance, do you?" he shook his head slowly. "No… with *your* wings, you wouldn't have to…"

I wasn't sure what he was muttering about, but I was already pretty exhausted. I figured the best course of action was just to let DinoHyde work things through at his own pace. When he was ready to share with me, he would. In the meantime, I wanted to rest up. Little did I know I'd need all the rest I could get.

Chapter Twenty One

The chilly night air burned its way down my throat. I was sitting on top of an abandoned building, my new feet accessories hanging off the edge. DinoHyde, ever vigilant, was standing a few yards away, glowering intently at the building across the road.

Get this, it was raining. I couldn't stop remembering the last time I sat in the rain waiting for something to happen.

I had already "observed" my end of the building about three times over. But once you witness two boring guys in suits signing papers greedily once, you really don't need to see it again to get the full experience.

DinoHyde pushed me for the entire day after using the Punchers. And then that whole night too. He insisted I learn basic self-defense, and then he wanted me to learn how to use the *endless* features of the helmet. *And then* he had me tripping all around his workshop in the prototype HawkBoots, as he called them, to make sure I'd be ready to use them out in the field.

Walking in the HawkBoots was not fun. The metal cylinders chaffed something fierce, not to mention the metal feet had *zero* traction against

DinoHyde's concrete floors. It ended up I had to cheat and half fly myself around the room just to move. I know I'm complaining but at the time… I kinda liked them. They made me a bit taller, and moving with my wings unfurled… I don't know, it just felt *right*. Like I could tell, even back then, that the HawkBoots would become my primary weapon.

To DinoHyde's credit, he added proper hawk-like claws to the ends that could lock or unlock on command from the R-MIG, which was just about the only part of the prototype HawkBoots that actually worked the way it was supposed to.

After that, I got a good… four-and-a-half hours of sleep before DinoHyde and I went on our first patrol.

I turned my attention back to the two suits passing paperwork around. They'd upgraded to *leaning over a desk*… while signing papers greedily…

Riveting stuff.

"Hey, can't you at least explain what we're watching?" I asked DinoHyde, breaking radio silence not for the first time that night.

"Coms are for emergencies," DinoHyde growled back weakly. He still hadn't switched his voice modulator on. I briefly wondered if that was intentional, or if he just forgot he'd turned it off.

"But I still don't know who these guys are or what they're doing," I squawked in protest. "How am I supposed to keep an eye out when I don't know what I'm looking for?"

"You're looking at Deric Mayborn and Jake Trapper. The bald one, Jake, is Barron Corps liaison to the bank. Deric, however, is a low-level asset manager for Barron Corps. As for what they're doing, they're illegally laying off fifty employees, while stealing millions of dollars of corporate funds."

I whistled. "That's impressive."

"This is what real crime looks like," DinoHyde said. "There's no thugs or back alleyways. Just office rooms and paper cuts."

"So how do we fit into this?" I asked, finally daring to get excited.

"Right now, we don't."

My squawk of protest caused him to jerk in pain.

"Patience," he told me irritably. "When one of them leaves, one of *us* will sneak in and steal the data off the hard drive, while the other of us will tail them to their home and attempt to take the paper copies. We can then leak them to the police and call it a night without anyone getting hurt."

"Really, so that's all we have to do?"

"That's it. One quick sneak and we save fifty people their jobs and put the bad guys behind bars. You don't get much more heroic than that."

"I don't know… It doesn't sound too exciting."

"Rookie…" DinoHyde said seriously, "Exciting means you messed up. Exciting means you have to fight, and fighting means you bleed. If you bleed—"

"Yeah, yeah. 'If you bleed you die.' You've given me this speech before. Now, who's going to raid the computers and who's going to tail the perp?"

"That depends. How much do you know about computers?"

"I know enough to stick the bug in the USB port," I scoffed.

Immediately, DinoHyde cringed. "That settles it, you tail the perp. Tomorrow, I'll teach you the basics of hacking."

I'm not going to lie, if his lessons on computers were in any way similar to his lessons on combat, the thought of taking computer lessons from DinoHyde made my stomach churn.

"Okay," I conceded. "So, I wait for someone to leave with the briefcase and I swoop in and-"

"No!" DinoHyde growled. "You can't just take it from the bad guys. That's stealing."

"What's the difference?!" I spluttered into the com.

"The difference is that my way, no-one sees your face. If we do it right, nobody will think a third party is involved. Just a bunch of crooks who made a mistake.

"If you jump in there all flying and bravado, these worms will yell 'Lawyer' and go right back to business as usual within the hour."

"That's insane!"

"That's life," DinoHyde punctuated his sentence with a truly fantastic growl that brooked no arguments. The silence between us was only interrupted by the sounds of a police siren in the distance. I remember looking away from

DinoHyde, thinking about that siren and how DinoHyde made no move to address it. I felt… grounded. Trapped. I was resigned to having one long night of boring work, and I had to take it on faith that DinoHyde was right and we really were doing what was best for everyone.

And… after my solo disasters… I was ready to take a few things on faith.

There was a movement in the offices. A security guard made his rounds and waved the two workers out of their cubicles.

"Good," DinoHyde said. "Keep your eyes on the briefcase—Don't let it out of your sight."

I promised that I wouldn't let him down.

"While you're stalking him, make sure you have a few feathers ready. Just in case he tries to fight you."

"I've got it covered," I confirmed seriously. "I brought this just in case." From my pockets, I withdrew the water gun I'd found in FabMaster's lair.

DinoHyde did a double-take when he saw it. "That's *mine!*" He hissed. "Where did you get that!"

"I found it."

"Where?!? I've been looking for that water gun ever since FloodGate stole the shrink-space prototype!"

"I just found it in a box in FabMaster's lair."

That seemed to stun DinoHyde more than anything else. "You know where FabMaster's lair is?"

"Y-yeah? You don't, I take it?"

"No… I was never invited in, even during the Great Corporate War. Back then, all the vigilantes stole my technologies."

"So that's how HotShot Lagoon made his invisible cowl!"

DinoHyde looked away, his tail drooping.

"What?" I asked, sensing the mood shift.

"I didn't… he… HotShot actually made that one before I did."

I was floored by the absurdity. DinoHyde was jealous! Oh, that put me in a strangely good mood to see the vigilante knocked down a peg.

I would've *loved* to continue this conversation, but, as luck would have it, the two businessmen exited the building right then. One of them, Deric Mayborn, carried the briefcase.

"Go, I'll catch up to you as fast as I can," DinoHyde commanded, taking charge of the situation again. "Take the gun, for now. You may need it if things go sour. We'll talk more about it later."

I gave him a sarcastic salute and flew off into the night.

I had a briefcase to steal.

Chapter Twenty Two

"Dino, buddy. We've got a problem."

I was conserving energy. Deric Mayborn was taking his sweet time walking home, so, instead of flying pointless circles around the guy and blowing my cover, I was walking across the rooftops, only taking flight to move from one to the next.

"I know we had a problem, but how do *you* know we've got a problem?" DinoHyde said.

"What?"

I could hear DinoHyde sigh through the coms. He really did design these things well.

"I'm on the computers now, but I'm not seeing any of their activities on the hard drive. No employees are getting laid off, and no money was transferred out of the corporate account. They didn't even print any of their paperwork here. It looks like Jake accessed his computer files remotely, but all that data is stored on the bank's servers."

I paused mid-flap to consider his words. "I thought that was illegal," I whispered frantically.

"It is. Give me a minute. I want to know why two upstanding gentlemen such as these were accessing bank servers remotely in the dead of night."

"That explains my problem… or at least, part of it."

"Why, what's wrong?"

"I recognize where I'm at. Deric Mayborn isn't going home tonight. He's meeting someone in the Heap."

"Hold back for now," DinoHyde whispered urgently. "Put some distance between you and Mayborn. Watch only. Do you copy? No matter what happens, stick to the shadows, and *do not engage*. I'm cracking the bank's firewall right now. It'll take a few minutes, but once we know what we're up against, I'll join you. We'll work this out together."

I nodded, completely forgetting that DinoHyde couldn't see me. "Right—uh—*roger that*… stay back and watch only." I was already planning on doing that much already.

A few blocks later, Mayborn went walking down a dark alleyway and ducked into a dilapidated building. I recognized the place. Square Court Plaza. It was once a decent apartment building in the area, but the gangs killed the owners after they refused to pay protection money. The building's luck only went downhill from there.

But… if I remembered correctly, it would have one very useful advantage for me.

Square Court Plaza got its name for the shape of its apartments. The building was built as one big square overlooking a small courtyard. Perfect for a winged superhero to do some subtle reconnaissance.

Contrary to popular belief, I don't *always* rush into things recklessly. In this case, I contacted DinoHyde with the location and my plans. He approved, but urged me to take the utmost caution. In other words, he told me it was a terrible idea, but he didn't tell me *not* to do it, so I did it anyway.

As fast as a sparrow, I darted across the empty street. I landed on the Plaza's roof as lightly as a butterfly. It's strange, now that I'm thinking back on it, how the clunky, metallic HawkBoots never seemed to feel quite so heavy to me when I was in the thick of the action. I realize in retrospect that… no… That's an entirely different rabbit hole to jump down… If I'm still alive in the morning, I'll tell you about it then. For now, the only relevant thing you need to know is that, while I was walking around as the Wingman, the HawkBoots never made a sound, and I never noticed them on my feet.

I crawled my way to the edge of the roof and peaked down into the courtyard below.

I didn't like the scene that greeted me.

Five armed thugs, each one carrying an Uzi, and one of them, taller and with a military crewcut, had an old M27 IAR on his back. For those of you who don't know, this was not your standard-issue thug guns. These Barron Corps creeps didn't play around with their mercenary budget.

When you live in a constant gang war, you get to know your guns… whether you want to or not. An Uzi is just slang for a fast-shooting, automatic weapon. Don't ask me why. They shoot fast, but are terribly wasteful. Great if you want to kill someone fast and don't care about how many bullets it takes, but the more *refined* goon for hire will tell you they're just noisemakers.

The M27, on the other hand… That's military hardware. And a classic one to boot. You didn't get one of those just anywhere. The other four goons sat there looking smug and confident. But Crewcut sat at the edge of the courtyard, eyeing the others disdainfully. I didn't know it at the time, but this man was the Grenadier. His custom M27 and I would cross paths many times over the years. The man was fond of his explosives, and he was very good at setting them in the most unlikely of places.

Like on the backs of four hostages sitting directly in the center of a courtyard with the other four thugs pointing their guns at them.

"Dino, I think I have an even bigger problem," I whispered urgently.

"I know, I see them too. I'm on my way now. It's rough, but, whatever you do, *stay hidden*. They cannot know you're there."

"But-"

"No exceptions. Remember rule two? Follow it."

"Was that the one about never talking, or never getting caught?"

"Damnit, bird-brain! This is serious. You need to wait for backup."

"Fine!" I fumed quietly, a hollow feeling sinking into my gut.

Four hostages. It was a family. A mom, a dad, and two kids. The "perfect nuclear family" that the media is so obsessed with. The children couldn't be any older than ten. The children were gagged and crying…

I…

…

I was clenching my fists.

The door to the lobby opened with a dramatic creak. Deric Mayborn walked in, all full of pomp and swagger. "Ah, Mr. Dawson, thank you so much for waiting." The nerd sounded just as weasely as he looked.

"Bastard," the hostage swore. "I'll kill you, you sonofa b—"

The Grenadier smacked Mr. Dawson with the butt of his M27. "That's enough of that," he said in a voice so torn up he growled worse than DinoHyde. He held up a small black box with four bright red buttons on it. "You don't want your pretty little family to die horrifically, do you?"

Mr. Dawson's bitter retort was lost to Mayborn's shrill giggling. "Tisk, tisk," he said once he'd caught his breath. "Such violence. A stand-up gentleman such as yourself should know better than to accept a loan from gangsters."

"Please, this is a mistake!" Mrs. Dawson pleaded in a voice that I can only describe as a "Karen voice." Like at any second she was about to demand to speak to Mayborn's manager. "We haven't taken a loan from anyone," she continued briskly.

"Really?" Mayborn exclaimed with false sincerity. He snatched the detonator from the Grenadier's hand and knelt between Mrs. Dawson and her children. The little girl whimpered into her gag again. Mr. Dawson struggled against his bonds, but the Grenadier stopped him cold by planting his gun right between Mr. Dawson's eyes.

Mrs. Dawson tried to lean away from Mayborn. He grabbed her by the hair and pulled her back. She choked back a sob. Her eyes were wide with terror.

"My files say otherwise," Mayborn whispered. The tension was so tight I could hear him from my perch three stories above them.

"Your files are wrong," she insisted defiantly.

"Mrs. Dawson!" Mayborn exclaimed sarcastically. He looked about conspiratorially. "Forging bank documents is a crime!" He said matter-of-factly. "Why, you could go to jail!"

The four thugs chuckled and japed with one another. Even the Grenadier managed to crack a smile.

I don't remember grasping the edge of the balcony, but I remember looking down and realizing I had such a vice-grip on the rail I could've ripped it off and threw it at them.

I *wanted* to rip the rail off and throw it at them…

But I held back.

"You should've sold your house when you had the chance," Mayborn continued. "If you had, you would have had all kinds of money when Mr. Dawson over here got laid off. You could've had a nice apartment, plenty of food. You wouldn't have had to overdraw your credit cards."

"What are you on about?" she snapped. "None of that happened— oh," she breathed, realization dawning on her face.

"You finally get it do you?" Mayborn jeered in the most asinine, condescending tone possible. "Let's just make sure, shall we? From the top. *This* is the signature of my colleague from the bank, Jake Tapper. He assures me, your finances have been messed up for months."

Mrs. Dawson recoiled as Mayborn spun his disastrous tale of shame and poverty.

Over my com's, I heard DinoHyde musing to himself. "So, it's a housing scheme. This is perfect. I've cracked the bank's computers and downloaded the files. Once I get there, we can nail these bastards to the wall. There's no telling how long they've run this game. They could have thousands of victims.

"Devil Chicken, you *need* to keep those thugs trapped in the Plaza. There are three exits. You need to seal them off, now."

But I wasn't paying attention to him. See, I realized something. Something DinoHyde missed. My body was shivering, down to my toes and across my wings. I prayed I was wrong.

But I wasn't.

The Dawson's could *see* Mayborn. They wouldn't be allowed to live.

Mayborn stood upright and kicked Mr. Dawson over on his side. "It's up to you boys," he said, gesturing between the thugs and the hostages, "quick or personal?"

"Personal, boss!" One of them exclaimed, the other three quickly asserted their agreements. Only the Grenadier looked disappointed. Mayborn tossed the detonator back to the Mercenary and pulled out a small pistol. He cocked the gun. And pointed it at Mrs. Dawson. "Say 'goodnight,' mommy," he laughed cruelly.

Mrs. Dawson only cried. Her daughter and husband tried to struggle once more. Her son had fallen over with his eyes screwed shut.

The gun's hammer pulled back.

But it never fired.

I made sure of it.

My body acted without needing my mind to tell it what to do. I wanted to stop this scene so badly... I should've jumped in long before now.

DinoHyde told me that people would only be surprised by something *once*. So I decided to make that "once" count. As quick as a falcon, I swooped down the three stories, less flying and more guided-falling. At the last second, I flared my wings and flipped the HawkBoots around to smash Mayborn's back into the concrete.

I drew in as big of a breath as I could and shrieked at the top of my lungs. DinoHyde's R-MIG system translated the shriek through the voice modulator and turned it into a booming squawk that made everyone clench their ears except me.

Rule Three. Check.

Now to figure out Rule Four. What was one move I could make to win? Easy.

Before the bad guys could recover, I launched myself at the Grenadier and pulled the detonator right out of his hand.

One of the thugs started shooting his Uzi wildly. What he was aiming for was anyone's guess. His shots flew so wildly, he clipped one of his buddies. It was only a matter of time before he got one of the hostages.

I scooped up all four of the Dawson's and launched myself straight up. It felt like my arms would tear themselves out of their sockets, but I managed to go four stories straight up before we tumbled onto a balcony.

For those of you at home, never try to move a person strapped to a bomb. I was damn lucky none of them exploded from the movement. I bet their lives that the only trigger was the detonator. That was not a gamble I should've made, but it all worked out… this time.

Anywho… Back to the action. Four stories, out of six… I didn't have the strength to do another jump. That… and I'm not quite sure how I managed to grab two people in each arm. I mean, yes. I just did it… but my brain was still trying to catch up to the last five seconds.

The thugs below were recovering. "They're still here, search the building!" the Grenadier snarled.

All of a sudden, I was sweating up a monsoon. My breath came out in ragged puffs on par with a drunken hobo who was forced to run a marathon… Come to think of it, that metaphor was kinda on the nose.

I couldn't run. I couldn't fight. That left one option: hide.

I plucked a larger feather from my wings and jammed the point in between the door and its frame.

"What's going on? Who are you?" Mr. Dawson sounded panicked. To be fair, he landed on his side, so he couldn't see anything.

"Stay calm, I'm a good guy," I told them soothingly. My modulator translated that into a light crooning tone that helped me just as much as it did them. "A-are you DinoHyde?" one of the kids whispered excitedly. I didn't have the time to answer.

The sound of thugs running up the stairs put a little more urgency back to my actions. I heaved my weight against the feather and used it as a crowbar to create a bit of space between the door and its frame. Reversing the feather in my hand, I used the sharp edges to saw through the security bar.

Propping the door open, I urged the Dawsons to run inside the room—after I cut off their bomb vests.

Another side note. Don't cut a bomb vest unless you're a trained professional. Again, I was damn lucky the Grenadier was lazy this time. I could've very easily blown all five of us straight to Hell.

The newly freed family reunited in the room I'd opened. There was a lot of hugging and non-fear related crying. I'd go into more detail, but my own mind was preoccupied with keeping the thugs off their backs. I was still holding the detonator in my hand—when I had an idea.

Leaving the Dawsons with instructions to remain as quiet as they could be, I shut them in the room. From the outside, their room looked just like any of the others. I doubt any of the thugs would be able to see any of the scratches and marks I'd made with it being so dark.

I grabbed the bomb vests and set my trap.

When the thugs reached my floor, I activated all four of the bombs, collapsing the entire stairwell and trapping all six of the bad guys on the third floor. From here, it was a simple matter of incapacitating them.

In keeping with the spirit of Rule number two, I slipped down the balcony and picked them off from behind. Two of the thugs lay unconscious in the rubble. But the Grenadier had good instincts. He'd stayed behind and subsequently avoided the rubble. Unfortunately for him, he decided to look at the damage first before trying one of the other stairwells. I had just enough room to arc the HawkBoots around and smack him on the back of the head with a satisfying *clang*!

The other two thugs didn't know what hit them. Dazed and confused, they came crawling out of the stairwell and stumbled right past me and the Grenadier without pausing. I flipped the first one off the ledge and the second *into* the drywall where he struggled uselessly to free himself.

That left one last person.

Deric Mayborn was currently trying to flee from the Plaza as fast as he could. I put an end to that by launching a big gust of wind with my wings. Not only did he flip up and over from the pressure, but his hand separated from the briefcase he was carrying.

I casually walked up and claimed the briefcase for my own. Tutting at Mayborn like a naughty child. Mayborn looked up at my wings and passed out.

I joined the Dawsons in their room at about the same time the cops started flashing their siren. Flooding the whole ground floor of the Plaza with red and blue lights.

"Go on," I urged. "You're free now. Here," I pushed the briefcase full of paperwork into Mr. Dawson's hands. "The papers in there should have you covered for the biggest lawsuit this country's ever seen."

"Thank you!" Mr. Dawson cried. "You saved us all. We owe you our lives. I'll never forget this for as long as I live!"

"That's fine," I said, not unkindly. "Just go now, get to the cops, and don't look back."

I didn't stay to see Dawson's reunion with the police, but I *did* catch the daughter explaining to the cops how DinoHyde had wings "this big" with her arms stretched all the way out. It brought a chuckle to me.

I'd saved them. I caught them before they fell. I… I cannot to this day tell you how happy it made me feel. For the first time since Jerry died in a gang shooting, I felt whole again.

Now I just had to meet up with DinoHyde.

Chapter Twenty Three

"YOU DID *WHAT* WITH THE FILES?!?" DinoHyde roared.

So much for my good feeling. I missed it already.

"I gave it to the Dawsons so they can keep their house."

DinoHyde grit his teeth so loudly I could hear it in the headset. "The Dawsons would've kept their house *anyway*. There was no need to hand over our bargaining chip."

"I don't get what the big deal is. The Dawsons will hand the files over to their lawyers and the cops will mop up the rest. That's the same end goal!"

"No. It's not."

"I don't follow."

DinoHyde sighed to himself. "I should've known this would happen. It's that damned rookie optimism. I should've been there. I should've made sure we did it right. I got cocky…"

I flexed my wings at him.

"I did NOT just fight off a bunch of thugs to get shamed on by you! I did one helluva good job back there. Five guys—with guns. Four hostages—with bombs. And I *nailed it!*"

DinoHyde growled in response. "There's always guys with guns!" he snarled. Bursting my sense of accomplishment. "There's always hostages and bombs. And you didn't 'nail it,' you got lucky! Lucky the mercenaries didn't think to set off the bombs at the first sight of you. Lucky the vests weren't motion-sensitive. Lucky that no one in that room had ever seen the likes of you before!

"You had no plan. No strategy. You didn't wait for backup. And worst of all, you handed over the one thing that was important, the one thing that could've landed everyone in this scandal in jail— permanently —to a middle-class paper pusher because his little girl was crying! And you think you should be congratulated? NO! You just put a target on their backs for the next eight months. Meanwhile, every rich fat-cat whose hands were caught in this cookie jar is going to set their alibis and pay off anyone it'll take to keep their names out of it.

"You saved *one* family. But if we'd done it my way, we would've saved thousands—and stopped this scandal for good!"

I don't know what I could've said to that. Even in retrospect, DinoHyde's speech hit me *hard*. I never forgot it. I was so eager to make a difference that I didn't really look at my actions, or how they'd impact people in the future. I was crushed. And I'd resent this moment for a long time to come.

But I don't regret it. I never have and I never will. Even now, I'm sure I did the right thing.

"The Dawson's would've died if I hadn't done something." I looked DinoHyde straight in the eye. And *he* looked away.

"I've done this job for a long time, rookie. The first and hardest lesson you learn is that you can't save everyone. Sometimes the victims have to die."

I couldn't believe my ears.

"A-are you telling me… No! That's not right! Hero's are supposed to save people!"

"Heroes are supposed to save *everyone*!" DinoHyde countered, waving my disgust away with a flick of his tail. "If you'd died trying to save one family, what then? How many hundreds of people would you save in your death?

Martyrs leave legacies. Vigilantes only leave corpses for our enemies to desecrate."

"You're telling me saving people is the wrong thing?"

"I'm telling you not to die needlessly! We're not gods. We bleed. And because we bleed, we die. We have to be better than ordinary people. We have to be symbols.

"We work in the shadows, moving blocks behind the scenes until the bad guys are all put away. If you do it right, no-one in the world will ever know your name, *Pollo Diablo*. They stop seeing you as a person and start fearing you. They believe in the impossible and crime rates plummet.

"To that end… sometimes you need to let a famil—"

"*Dawson's*," I squawked. "That's their names. They're not 'the victims,' or 'the hostages.' They're the Dawsons. Paul and Mary Dawson with their children Fred and Sara. They're middle-class workers who just wanted to keep the house they live in."

DinoHyde still wouldn't meet my eyes. His tail swished angrily, which was the only indication that he'd even heard me at all.

"..."

"..."

I glared back at him.

"Getting attached..." DinoHyde couldn't finish his sentence.

"I'm going to get attached," I leered threateningly. "To each and every damn person in this hellhole of a city. I'm going to learn their names, and what makes them tick. And their favorite color, and their dog's names and... and—"

DinoHyde choked. His voice, when he spoke again, didn't sound quite so commanding anymore. "You're just going to get hurt. Your heart's going to bleed until you die."

"It's better than whatever happened to you," I retorted.

DinoHyde didn't answer that right away, either. He stepped away and looked out at the rising sun. "Old age happened to me, rookie. You may not like it, but, if you're lucky, it'll happen to you too."

The silence grew between us as the sun rose higher into the sky. Cars rushed past us on the roads below. Early morning. Most people were still in bed.

I remembered when I walked those streets while I was mourning Sam Farsight. So much had changed so fast since then.

I didn't feel like Sam anymore. The costume, the gadgets… even the wings… those were all just window dressings. I was different from the scared little boy who wanted to start a gang war. I didn't know who I was yet. But I knew who I wasn't.

"I don't think I'm cut out to be your apprentice… not yet… maybe not ever."

DinoHyde, his back to me, straightened his posture slightly. I was starting to get the feel for how he operated. I understood that what I just said hurt him more than anything else that'd happened tonight. But he'd never show it as pain. DinoHyde would die before he'd let anyone witness him bleed.

"Think it over, take a few days," DinoHyde said. He still wasn't using his voice modulator. I could hear the slight variation of tones in his voice that give away when someone's barely holding it together. "I'll contact you… If you're still sure…"

"We'll talk about it," I promised. But even as I flew away… I knew. I wasn't DinoHyde, and I never would be. I was something altogether new.

I took off after that.

I didn't know what else to do. I spent that first day in a bit of a shock. I switched my hero suit for the hobo suit and panhandled for a bit… My heart wasn't in it. I just kept looking at everybody and wondering if they would want me to save them. I kept seeing all the stuck up soccer moms walk their kids in a safe, twelve-foot radius around me, and I could just imagine them saying, *not this one, children. If you're ever in danger, wait for the Runner to show up.* And after about seven instances of this… I was starting to agree with them.

I was a farce.

Pollo Diablo; Devil Chicken… Sam Farsight, the Pigeon… I wasn't a superhero.

I tried to think of even one instance where I hadn't made things worse. But the only example I could keep pointing to was the Dawsons…

To that end, sometimes you need to let a family die.

The words I never let DinoHyde finish speaking.

We're not gods, He'd said, *We don't decide who lives and who dies!*

...

But who does?

I'd never really been much for religion. Just a bunch of people locking the world away from them and convincing themselves they're better off if it burned without them. Not very cool. Being a hero was so much cooler.

But. Oh God, what if that's what it took to be a hero? Did I truly have the resolve to let a few people die so I could stop the bad guys?

No. That's not what I signed up for!

I couldn't take my thoughts anymore. After the sun started setting again with zero sleep in 48 hours, I decided to knock myself out... with some help.

Two months sober. Two months since I was in this hole-in-the-wall bar. Two months since my shoes stuck to the tacky floor, or since I smelled that graceful combination of booze and vomit. Two months of gaining back any dignity! Hello rock bottom, my old friend.

What else was I supposed to do?

What else *was* there for me to do?

I stared at the bottle all night, but not a drop touched my lips.

…

I couldn't do it.

That rabbit hole… I knew if I picked up that bottle one more time… I'd never get out of it. Damn it, it's supposed to be easy to be an addict, right? Try it once on a dare and never stop. That's the right way you ruin your life! So why couldn't I?

…

I know why I couldn't.

…

And I knew it at the time.

…

Being responsible… sucks.

On the second night of tempting myself, I threw the bottle away and ordered a soda.

I could've lost myself in a bottle again—I could've. But… I didn't really want that release. I wanted to be better. I wanted to *do* better. I didn't want to lose myself again; not when I was so close to finding myself.

"Ha, you are DD today, da?" The half Russian bartender laughed as I drank my soda angrily.

"Something like that," I muttered.

"Good," he nodded affirmatively. "We give discounts to DD—you buy dinner too, yes?"

…

How could I say no?

The next day, I patrolled as a hero. Nice and bright daylight; none of that cloak and dagger nocturnal stuff. There wasn't much to do, and my heart still wasn't up to investigating anything new.

It was a "Me Day," whoever I was.

I have to admit, I tee-totally forgot that I never went into the bar in my hero suit before. That was an… experience.

The bartender was the only one who took it in stride.

"Bwahaha," he laughed after I ordered another soda at the bar, my wings tucked princely over my shoulders. "So, this is what you're like without mask."

I swear the heart attack he gave me was more intense than any I would ever experience. My heart stopped for like, *a full minute*. That is, before I realized that my cowl was still firmly on my face. This, of course, brought out even more of a laugh from him.

"Y-you know who I am?" I asked.

"Of course!" he answered shamelessly. "You are wing man on the papers. And television. You are also drunk that came here for months. You refused to leave on Karaoke night."

My face burned from embarrassment. God only knows what expression showed on my cowl. "Yeah, that's me," I admitted, taking a sip from the soda he offered me.

The other patrons were eyeing me awkwardly, but, after a few drinks, even the most cautious of them ignored me. The barkeep, Isaiah Heiwajima, had an unusual knack for getting his way. Not that anyone would ever pick a fight with him. His two-piece suit with the sleeveless vest was almost as legendary as his Sushi Thursdays. Dude may have been from Japan (long story), but he was a brawler. He could smack heads with even the biggest of surly drunks that walked into his bar.

Lucky me, he seemed to think I was good for business. He spent the whole night telling patrons about my drunken exploits. "Remember that one night," he drawled on, "you pulled man out of tabletop."

"Yes," I said wearily for about the thousandth time. I thought once about leaving, Isaiah didn't seem to actually care about my answers, but, the one time I made a move for the door, he blocked me with a frighteningly forceful grip.

"Yes, he told story about his girlfriend breaking up with him, and you walked him around the whole night until he hit on a new girl."

"That… sounds like me."

"And then you proceeded to throw up over both of them. Ah, it was true love."

"…"

The night dawdled on. For my troubles, Isaiah made sure I was well fed. He even waved the bill for the night, saying that it was a special occasion. But… there was something about the way he said it that got me wondering if he knew, even then, that I was homeless. I'd never thought much about the bars I attended back when I was mourning. Just that the Spartanly named "Russia Hot-Wings," always seemed to have booze when everywhere else dried up. It felt like… Well, sitting there surrounded by other people like me, down on their luck with nothing and nowhere to go… It reminded me that I wasn't alone, and that I was far from hopeless. For a timeless minute that might've lasted a few hours, I knew why Isaiah stayed in his bar. He truly loved people. And seeing them there, at his bar, showed them at their best and worst. The alcohol revealed whatever had been hiding in them.

"Here, wing person," he called after the night had started wearing down. "I need help of DD."

I was baffled, at first, because I was so caught up in the moment that I thought he was about to regale me with another tale I'd graciously forgotten. But he was instead standing over a passed-out drunk who'd slumped out of his seat. Isaiah tapped the man on his face to rouse him, but, when he could only manage a slurred "whashyouupta," Isaiah patted down his pockets.

"This man come here alone. Come, I take keys, you take him home, yes?"

I rolled my shoulders noncommittally. "Don't you just toss them out?"

"Usually," he admitted. "But only if they don't pay. It's bad business to throw out well-mannered customers, you know."

After a few tries, Isaiah managed to get the drunk's address out of him. It was only a few blocks away.

"I guess I could fly him there," I agreed. At this, Isaiah's face lit up in horror.

"Good lord, no! No-fly. This man no good to fly. Walk him there, is much safer, yes?"

And this, children, is how I got myself roped into walking, arm in arm, with a drunken man, who smelled strongly of barbeque sauce, in the middle of the night, down the main road in the Heap, to a rundown apartment that had seen much better days.

"Thank you," the drunk said, almost non-stop. "You're a lifesaver, you know? A real hero."

"I try," I muttered wearily.

That night, I flew up to a random park and slept under a tree. It wasn't the most satisfying experience in the world. But I felt so much better than I did before.

Chapter Twenty Four

I was flying around when I heard the BOOM.

The rest of my day passed fairly uneventfully. I had a small nap on top of the Grier Building, and then I grabbed my stuff from their hiding place near FabMaster's lair. So much had happened since then, but a quick survey of my bag showed that no one had found my little hiding place. I used my toothbrush to brush my teeth and a small razor to shave, but I didn't change out of my suit. DinoHyde was still around somewhere and he'd want to meet soon.

Thing is, I didn't know where he wanted to meet. Between the darkness and the sewers (don't ask), I had no idea where DinoHyde's lair was. If he wanted to talk, he'd have to contact me on his own somehow.

Just as I was having that thought, a blast of noise hit me like a sack of bricks. With it came screaming, a wave of heat… and sirens.

I could see the smoke from miles away. Better than GPS for a hero in the sky. I arrived on the scene in less than a minute. A law office run by Puller & Gain had caught fire! Already the inferno consumed the top three floors and was quickly spreading to its neighbors!

I made to draw the watergun I'd kept with me. The pressure made me fumble around in my lower pockets blindly for a whole five seconds before I remembered I'd put it in one of my chest pockets.

Water gun in hand, I opened fire.

Calling FloodGate's pistol a "watergun" is a bit of an understatement. As DinoHyde briefly mentioned, it uses compressed space technology to make very big things fit into very small spaces… If I'd been paying attention, I would've remembered how "pressure" works. You see, I didn't fail physics. If I had remembered about pressure, I'd have known that firing that gun would send a shock-wave through my body, literally launching me through the air.

Unfortunately, I didn't think about any of that. The gun fired a stream of water so strong it punched a hole clean into the fourth floor. All that force also rebounded on me, forcing my arm and everything connected to it back into my wings…

All that to say, "I broke my wrist and dislocated my shoulder."

Yeah, so… once again, my first-attempt-curse made sure I messed it up as bad as I could.

Before I could properly congratulate myself for another job well done, a jet of fire came blasting out of the building. Clue one that this fire was unnatural. The stream of fire swiped left and right down the street below where the BCPD and the Fire Department were forming a line. Clue number two. From deep inside the room, a voice laughed. "You can't stop me now!" he shouted to the cops below. Clue three.

I was dealing with an arsonist.

The Arsonist continued to blast fire out of the hole I'd carved into the building. The flames were spreading fast. Other buildings were catching fire, and the Briar City Fire Department had their hands full trying to contain it.

There was a scream from inside the law office. "Shut up!" the Arsonist demanded. Followed a second later by another stream of fire from the window. "I have hostages!" The Arsonist shouted down to the cops. "Get me ten million dollars and a bagel, or I send them back to you in an urn!"

The cops, being cops, started to just bust in. I realized what was about to happen an instant before it happened.

The building's ground floor exploded.

I had only an instant to act, and I used it to swoop down and pull one lone cop away from the building. Sixteen other officers were not so lucky. Four of them only suffered extreme burns, but the rest…

The man I'd saved turned out to be none other than my rookie friend from the bank heist. "You!" he sputtered once he finally got his bearings.

"Yeah, me—Now look, I'm about to go in there and rescue those hostages. You need to go tell your captain, squad—whatever—to keep that firebug occupied."

"Don't think this makes us even!" the officer said, crawling to his feet in disgust. "The Catcher's going to chase you to the center of Hell and back."

"I'm counting on it," I said, brushing him off. "Just make sure you're ready when I give the signal."

"What signal?" The rookie shouted up uselessly as I took to the sky. The joke was on him though, I never had a signal. I just thought it sounded cool…

I entered the burning building on the fourth-floor, thinking to surprise the Arsonist and-slash-or steal his hostages—only to make a terrible discovery.

"Well, well. It looks like I caught a hero. I was hoping to catch one in blue; I wasn't expecting a cowl."

It was a trap.

Behind me, a part of the building collapsed over the hole I dove in through. In front of me, a stream of flames launched itself right at me!

I rolled to the side, my wings tucked close. I had no idea if they were fireproof or not, but the room was too narrow. Plus, whipping my wings around in this mess would only cause the flames to become even more unstable. My head was swimming from the heat and looking around the room was like being underwater. The air currents were bursting with energy, all going straight up!

Another piece of the roof collapsed, trapping me in a corner against the wall.

"Too easy!" the arsonist laughed. "There's not a person in the world who knows fire like I do. I've spent years kindling this flame. What made some nobody like you think you could step up to my plate?"

"I brought a cannon," I muttered. Remembering Martin's advice from long ago I held the gun in my left hand. Gritting my teeth, I forced my pained right arm to brace myself properly. Aiming for center mass, I opened fire with FloodGate's pistol, straight at where the voice was coming from.

Worked like a charm for half a second.

I heard the Arsonist swear as a blast of water and steam punched through the rubble blocking me with no more resistance than tissue paper. I dove through the hole I'd made, only to find a fresh wave of fire being blasted right at me!

I risked opening my wings enough to jump over it. The sharp updraft sucked me into the ceiling. But this was what I needed. With a proper foothold, I launched myself deeper into the center of the room.

This spot was the most controlled spot in the room. Fire along the walls and roof kept the edges of the room a minefield. Furthermore, it was built with thin half-walls to cordon off the employees from one another. Nothing but wood and paperwork; kindling and ash. Except for the center of the room.

I'd bet the Arsonist was waiting for me there. Lucky me, I was right.

He pulled the trigger on his contraption, and I hastily shot off another blast from FloodGate's pistol.

Ordinarily, water puts out fire like nobody's business. But the Arsonist wasn't using ordinary fire. DinoHyde reckoned later that he was using some kind of high-powered accelerant, based on how his fire-spewing contraption looked like a rifle with a few bulbs on the end.

Also, because it instantly evaporated my water blast.

The steam and pressure blew us both back towards opposite ends of the room. Each still keeping their weapons trained on the other. My right arm didn't want to keep holding the left, but I knew… if I dropped my guard for even a second, he'd burn me on the spot.

"I recognize you now," he spoke up. "You're that new one. Those wings look real to me. I bet they taste like chicken."

"You can't win this," I told him. He was stalling for time… but so was I. "The police are moving in as we speak."

"Ha," he scoffed. "You think those nitwits stand a chance? I already took care of all the exits. All they'll end up doing is adding more bodies to the oven."

"I'm going to stop you," I told him as calmly as I could. It was not as easy as it sounds. My heart was racing! The heat at my back was a constant pressure to *move*! But if I even tried, I'd become Barbeque. There was a time for action. But right now, I had to stay calm. My mind raced for anything to beat him. But I couldn't look away—even that action would be too much of an opening.

"You don't get it, meat. Even as we speak, the fire's getting higher and higher. The hostages are running out of air, and the smoke is filling up that tiny room. You can't beat me. Even if you do, the room's too hot to evacuate them before the building collapses. Just face facts. I've already won this one. You lost from the moment you stepped foot in here!"

That's when it hit me. He was right. I *had* lost. I'd lost my friends, my family… my dignity. I'd even lost my life. I wanted to save people. But all I'd been trying was picking fights. HotShot… DinoHyde. Cutter. I was trying so hard to prove that I could be a hero too, I forgot what it was I actually wanted to do.

No more kids in caskets.

That realization escaped me as a laugh. I couldn't help it! I'd been such an idiot up until then. I completely dropped my guard and succumbed to the insanity of it all.

This, at least, took the Arsonist by surprise. "What are you laughing at?" he demanded.

"It's nothing, nothing!" I chuckled, waving him aside. "I just realized something. That's all. I've been going about this all wrong. I just realized, we don't have to fight at all!"

"You're not going to fight me?" The look on his face was priceless. Hesitant, but thoroughly confused.

"No, I'm not going to fight you," I assured him. "You see, I don't have to. There's no point to it. All I have to do is put out the fire."

With that, I cracked FloodGate's pistol across my knee, breaking it open and releasing all the water it'd stored up.

Let me tell you, that was a lot of water!

It didn't matter how strong the Arsonist's contraption was, it couldn't hold up to a massive wave of water rushing him all at once. It knocked him out cold. The force of the flood was so strong that it completely blasted out the partitions and flowed out of the devastated walls and down the building. Putting out the fire, just as I'd hoped.

All that water pressure hit me point blank and blasted me right out into the streets. I pulled myself into the air easily enough, but the Arsonist would've died if I hadn't managed to catch him by his ankle. And yes, it was just as disgusting of a foot as you'd expect. If I wasn't preoccupied with making sure we didn't both smack the concrete at terminal velocity, I would've dropped him. Fortunately for me, (and *very* unfortunately for the Arson) I pulled out of the haphazard dive right in front of The Catcher.

"Freeze, Scum. You're under arrest." The Catcher had his gun pointed right at the Arsonist. The pomp was a touch unnecessary though, considering that between the water blast and the death defying fall the Arsonist was already passed out.

I smiled to myself. Because I *didn't* have to beat the bad guys. The Catcher would do it for me. That's what his job was. That's the job DinoHyde and HotShot Lagoon all signed up for. They could lock up all the bad guys they wanted.

All I had to do was catch them the next time the Sam Farsights of the world jumped off a building. The world—no, the *universe* would sort out the rest.

I came in for a gentle landing next to the Catcher. He couldn't catch me. Not today, not anyday. The rest of his troops were busy fishing the survivors out of the building. Even if he wanted to, the Catcher didn't have enough men with RPGs to stop me.

"Don't think this makes us even *Pollo Diablo*," he said. "I'm going to catch you too. If not today, then tomorrow."

"You can try," I said, tilting my head so one eye on my cowl blinked at him. "But you will *never* succeed. You can cuff my hands and bind my feet. You can burn me, stab me, shoot me, beat me down, and break every bone in my body. But you will never *catch* me.

"This city is my city. I will serve her to my death. I will save everyone in my reach. Especially the people you can't. I will support them all when things go bad… And carry the drunks home when they've lost their way. I'm this city's wingman. I will catch *every* person who falls. You cannot stop me. When this city spins herself into a mess, I'll always be right there to clean it up."

"I won't ever stop chasing you," he swore.

"That's fine." I insisted. "Do your best! And remember; I'm always around. Flying headfirst into the nearest disaster. No matter how dangerous."

"Because you think you're the city's *wingman*?" he returned sarcastically.

I flew up to him and put my beak right in his face. The pressure my wings created had to be unbearable. My feet, encased as they were in the HawkBoots, didn't even touch the ground. But to his credit, the Catcher never backed down. All he had to do was reach out and he could've put his cuffs around my wrists.

But he didn't.

"That's it exactly," I said. And flew away, deliberately dropping a single feather over the unconscious arsonist.

The next day, all the papers started calling me The Wingman. Over the next twenty years, that's exactly who I became. I was as good as my word—and then some.

… God, I wish I could've given a speech that good on TV.

Epilogue

DinoHyde was waiting for me on top of the Green Emperor. So much for him not knowing where FabMaster's lair was…

His arms were crossed.

"I told you not to do anything reckless!" he said. "That's all I asked for. Just cool your jets for a bit. What do I get instead? You jumped headfirst into a burning building! What do you *possibly* have to say for yourself?"

I turned away and tossed him my cowl. He didn't want to see my face, after all. "I'm not going to join you, DinoHyde," I said. "You and I are just too different. I know what I need to do now, and I won't need your tech to do it."

DinoHyde growled irritably. I could hear his tail sweeping across the rooftop. "You… you might as well keep the cowl," he said, almost reluctantly. "After that stunt, this thing's too hot. The world has seen you in it. If I ever use it again, people will know I gave it to you. If they knew I gave it to you, they'll know I have a network. They'll know I'm human, and that I can bleed."

"That's *such* a shame," I said, taking back the cowl and placing it firmly on my head. It already fit like a glove. But DinoHyde wasn't finished with me yet. While I tucked the flaps down into my suit, DinoHyde used that opportunity to step in front of me and give me his patented stare down.

"You're not like me. You don't have what it takes to get to the heart of the problem. You're content to lock up a few thugs, but you won't touch the big boys. And then you decide you're going to go flying half-cocked after every cat up a tree. If you don't get your head on straight, you're not going to last long. You'll burn out without making a real difference."

I laughed. The hood translated it into a shrill squawk that made DinoHyde back up a pace. "I'm not like you?" I japed. "That's the only thing you've *ever* said that I agree with! You're damn right, I'm not like you. You skulk around in the shadows, building yourself up like a god, while the victims eat lead for breakfast… All so *you* don't have to step into the daylight where the bad guys can see the seams in your costume.

"I'm not afraid to bleed. That's what makes me different."

9 781956 835991